HERE'S NEGAN!

THE WALKING DEAD

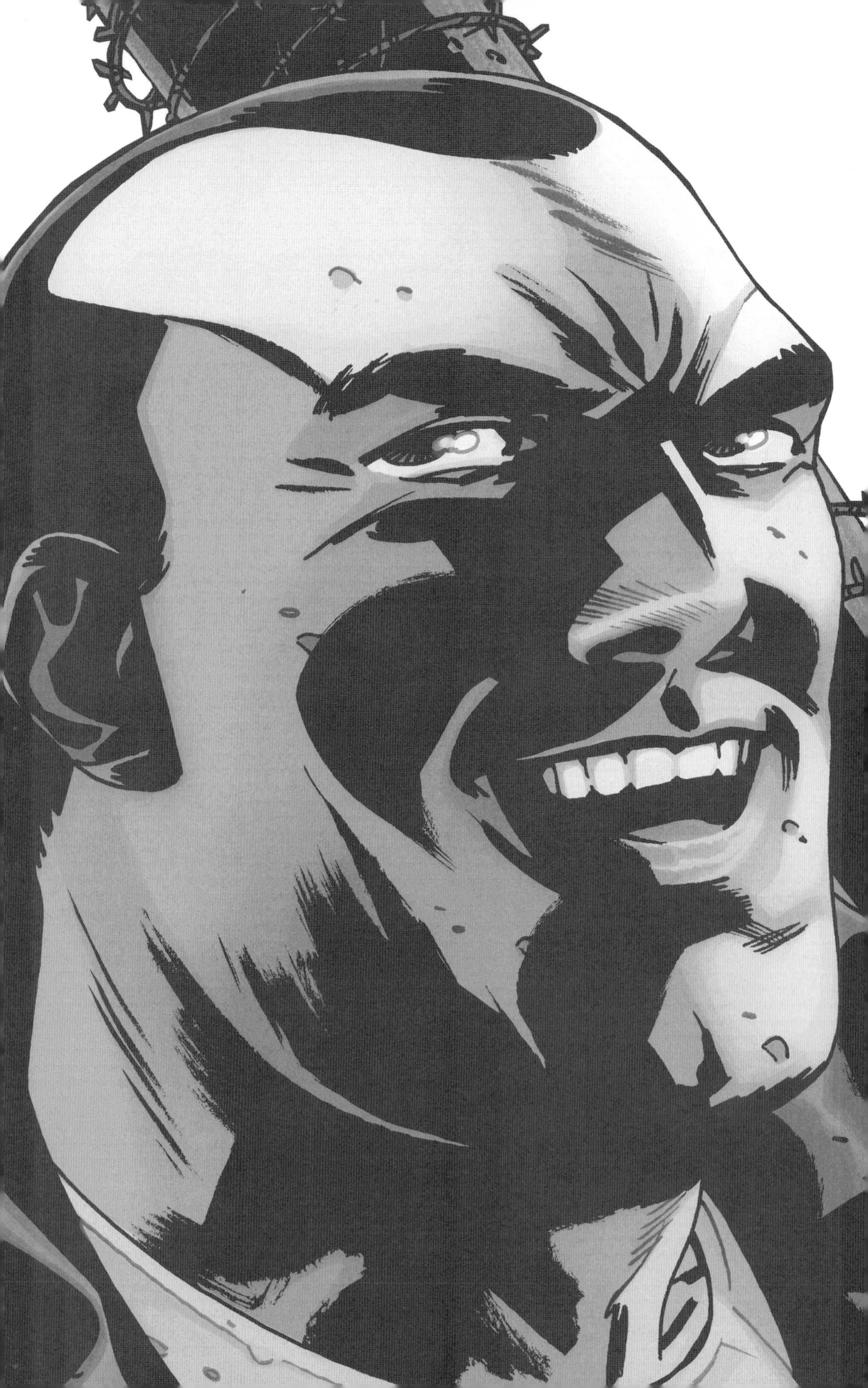

IMAGE COMICS PRESENTS

The Walking Dead

HERE'S NEGAN!

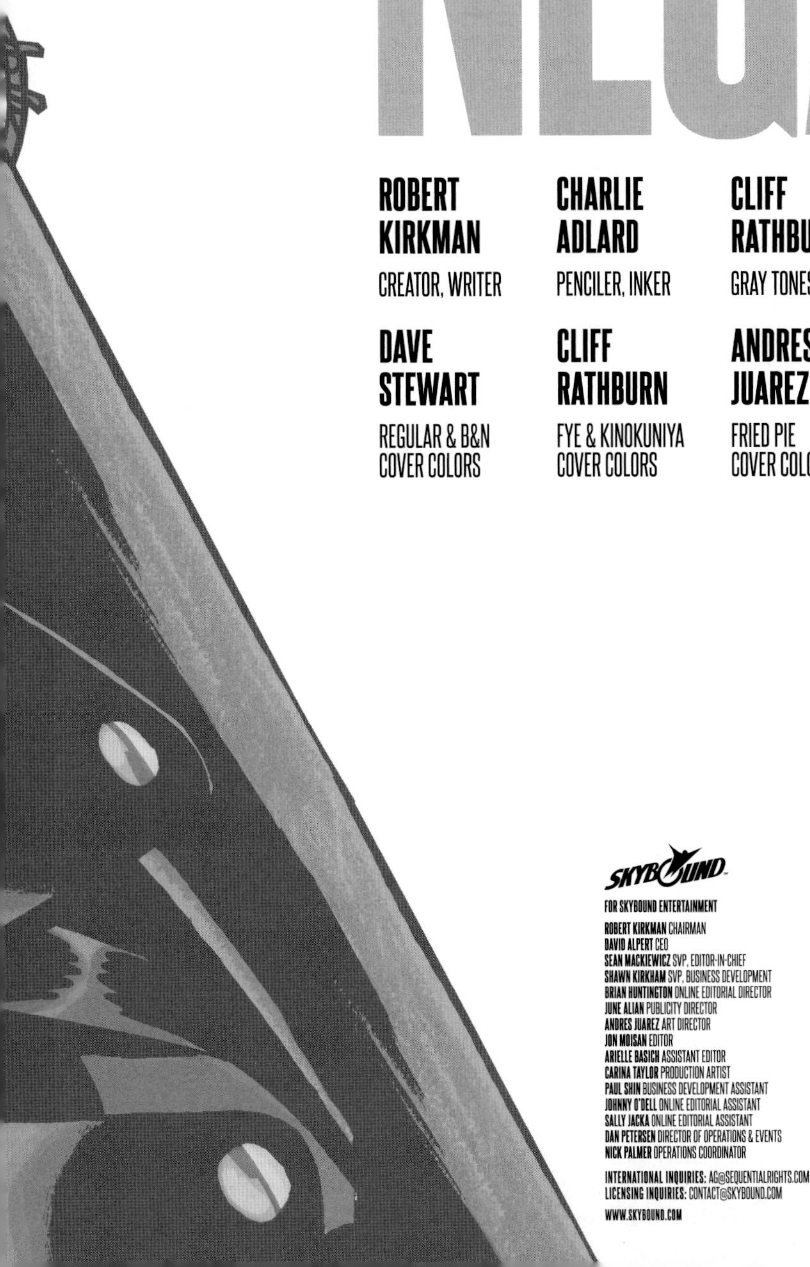

ROBERT KIRKMAN
CREATOR, WRITER

CHARLIE ADLARD
PENCILER, INKER

CLIFF RATHBURN
GRAY TONES

RUS WOOTON
LETTERER

SEAN MACKIEWICZ
EDITOR

DAVE STEWART
REGULAR & B&N COVER COLORS

CLIFF RATHBURN
FYE & KINOKUNIYA COVER COLORS

ANDRES JUAREZ
FRIED PIE COVER COLOR

FOR SKYBOUND ENTERTAINMENT

ROBERT KIRKMAN CHAIRMAN
DAVID ALPERT CEO
SEAN MACKIEWICZ SVP, EDITOR-IN-CHIEF
SHAWN KIRKHAM SVP, BUSINESS DEVELOPMENT
BRIAN HUNTINGTON ONLINE EDITORIAL DIRECTOR
JUNE ALIAN PUBLICITY DIRECTOR
ANDRES JUAREZ ART DIRECTOR
JON MOISAN EDITOR
ARIELLE BASICH ASSISTANT EDITOR
CARINA TAYLOR PRODUCTION ARTIST
PAUL SHIN BUSINESS DEVELOPMENT ASSISTANT
JOHNNY O'DELL ONLINE EDITORIAL ASSISTANT
SALLY JACKA ONLINE EDITORIAL ASSISTANT
DAN PETERSEN DIRECTOR OF OPERATIONS & EVENTS
NICK PALMER OPERATIONS COORDINATOR

INTERNATIONAL INQUIRIES: AG@SEQUENTIALRIGHTS.COM
LICENSING INQUIRIES: CONTACT@SKYBOUND.COM

WWW.SKYBOUND.COM

IMAGE COMICS, INC.

ROBERT KIRKMAN CHIEF OPERATING OFFICER
ERIK LARSEN CHIEF FINANCIAL OFFICER
TODD MCFARLANE PRESIDENT
MARC SILVESTRI CHIEF EXECUTIVE OFFICER
JIM VALENTINO VICE PRESIDENT

ERIC STEPHENSON PUBLISHER
COREY MURPHY DIRECTOR OF SALES
JEFF BOISON DIRECTOR OF PUBLISHING PLANNING & BOOK TRADE SALES
CHRIS ROSS DIRECTOR OF DIGITAL SALES
JEFF STANG DIRECTOR OF SPECIALTY SALES
KAT SALAZAR DIRECTOR OF PR & MARKETING
BRANWYN BIGGLESTONE CONTROLLER
KALI DUGAN SENIOR ACCOUNTING MANAGER
SUE KORPELA ACCOUNTING & HR MANAGER
DREW GILL ART DIRECTOR
HEATHER DOORNINK PRODUCTION DIRECTOR
LEIGH THOMAS PRINT MANAGER

TRICIA RAMOS TRAFFIC MANAGER
BRIAH SKELLY PUBLICIST
ALY HOFFMAN EVENTS & CONVENTIONS COORDINATOR
SASHA HEAD SALES & MARKETING PRODUCTION DESIGNER
DAVID BROTHERS BRANDING MANAGER
MELISSA GIFFORD CONTENT MANAGER
DREW FITZGERALD PUBLICITY ASSISTANT
VINCENT KUKUA PRODUCTION ARTIST
ERIKA SCHNATZ PRODUCTION ARTIST
RYAN BREWER PRODUCTION ARTIST
SHANNA MATUSZAK PRODUCTION ARTIST
CAREY HALL PRODUCTION ARTIST
ESTHER KIM DIRECT MARKET SALES REPRESENTATIVE
EMILIO BAUTISTA DIGITAL SALES REPRESENTATIVE
LEANNA CAUNTER ACCOUNTING ANALYST
CHLOE RAMOS-PETERSON LIBRARY MARKET SALES REPRESENTATIVE
MARLA EIZIK ADMINISTRATIVE ASSISTANT

WWW.IMAGECOMICS.COM

THE WALKING DEAD : HERE'S NEGAN. First Printing. Published by Image Comics, Inc., Office of publication: 2701 NW Vaughn St #780, Portland, OR 97210.

PRINTED IN USA. For information regarding the CPSIA on this printed material call: 203-595-3636 and provide reference #760941.
ISBN: 978-1-5343-0327-0 FYE ISBN: 978-1-5343-0590-8 KINO ISBN: 978-1-5343-0592-2
BN ISBN: 978-1-5343-0589-2 BAM ISBN: 978-1-5343-0591-5

HERE'S NEGAN!

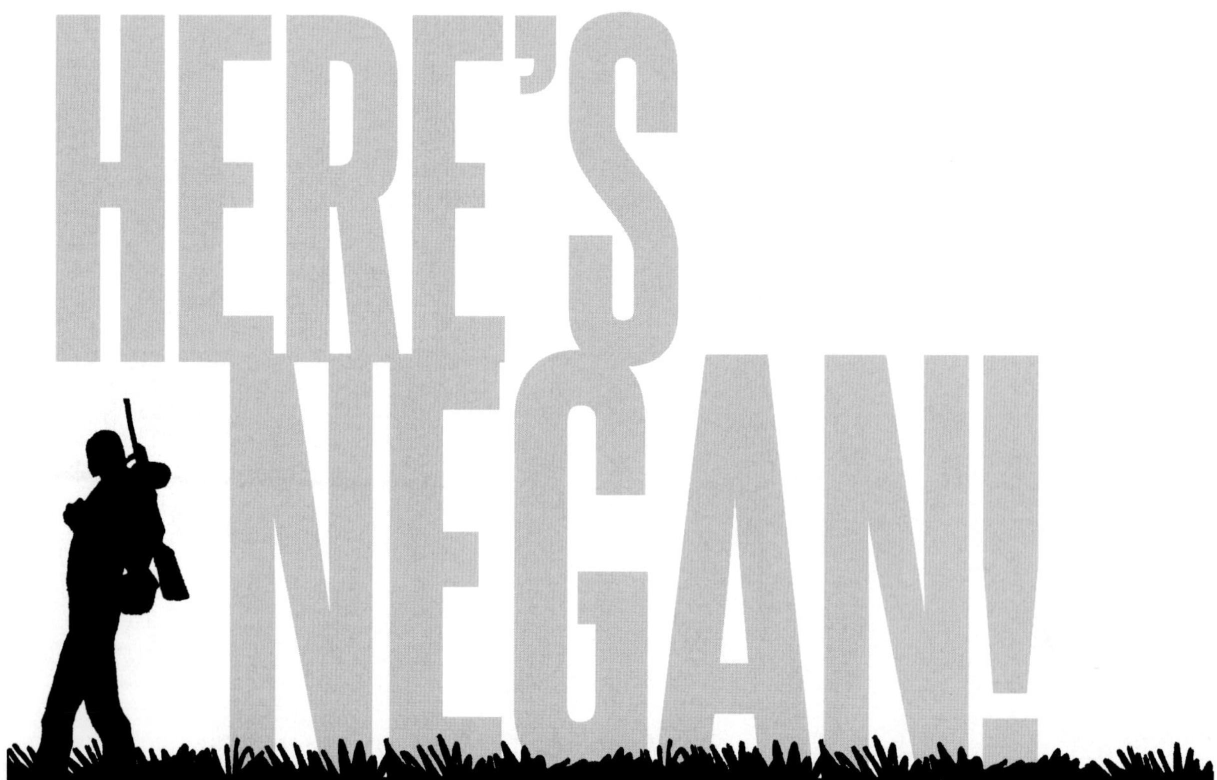

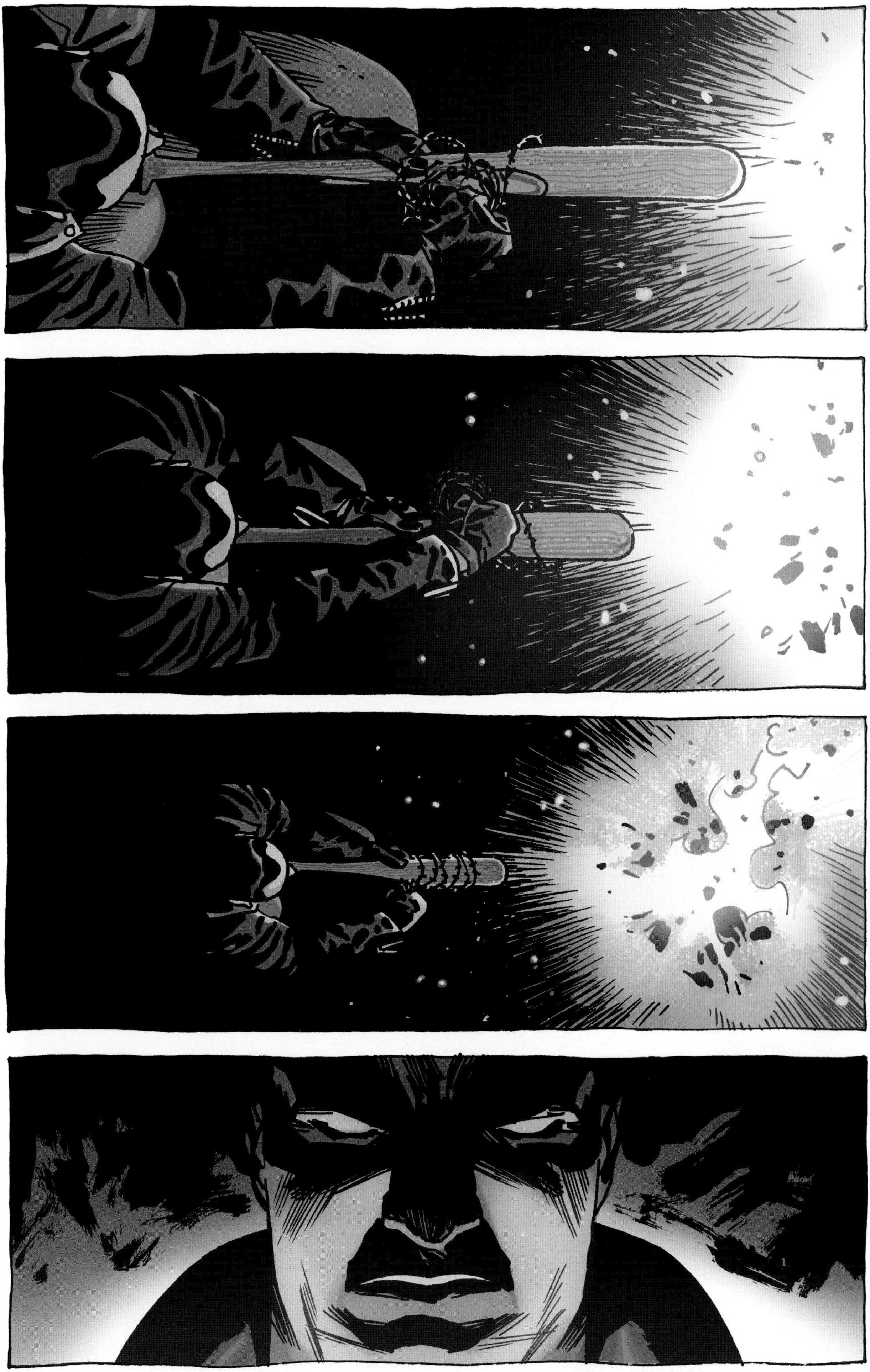

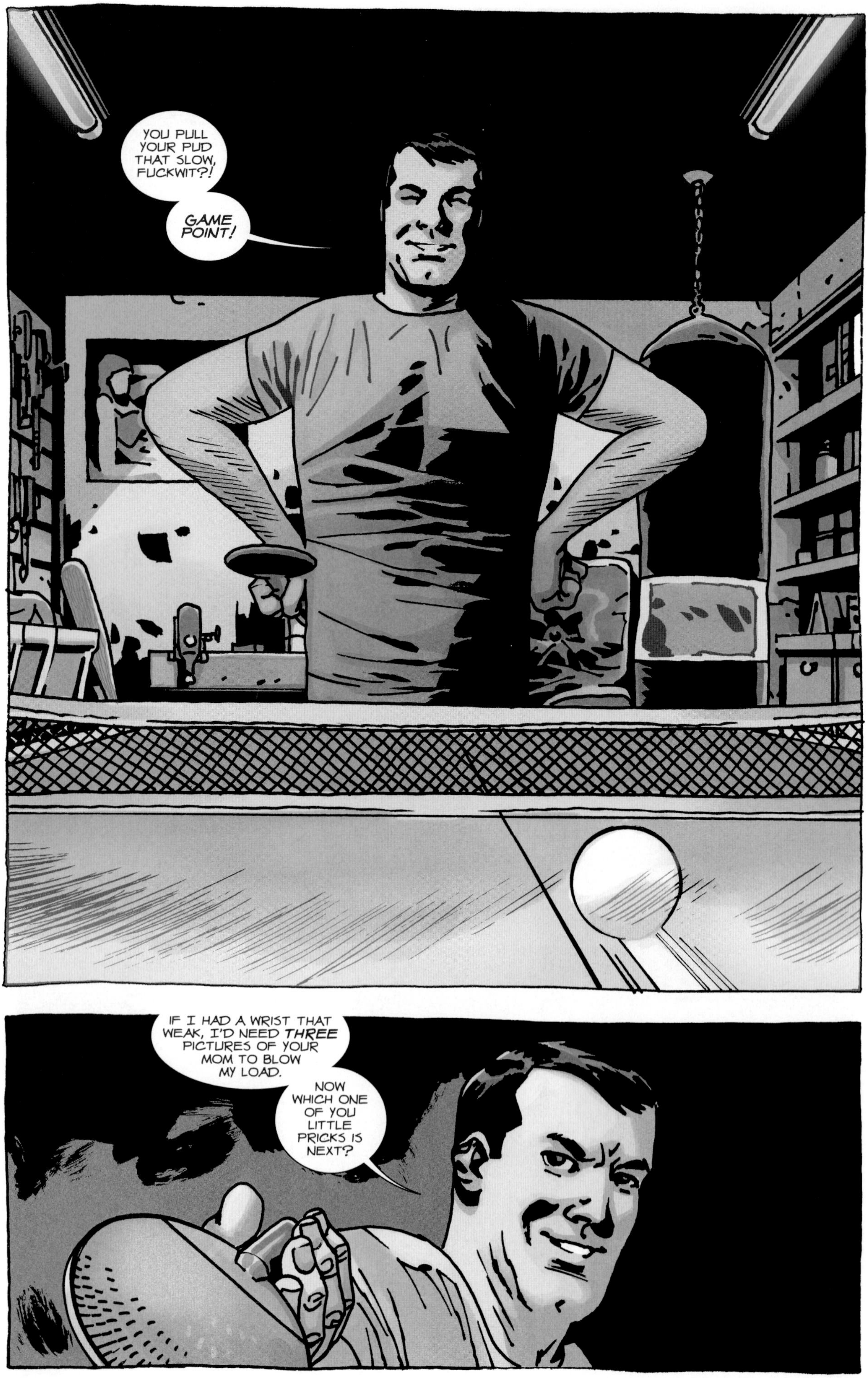

YOU PULL YOUR PUD THAT SLOW, FUCKWIT?!
GAME POINT!
IF I HAD A WRIST THAT WEAK, I'D NEED *THREE* PICTURES OF YOUR MOM TO BLOW MY LOAD.
NOW WHICH ONE OF YOU LITTLE PRICKS IS NEXT?

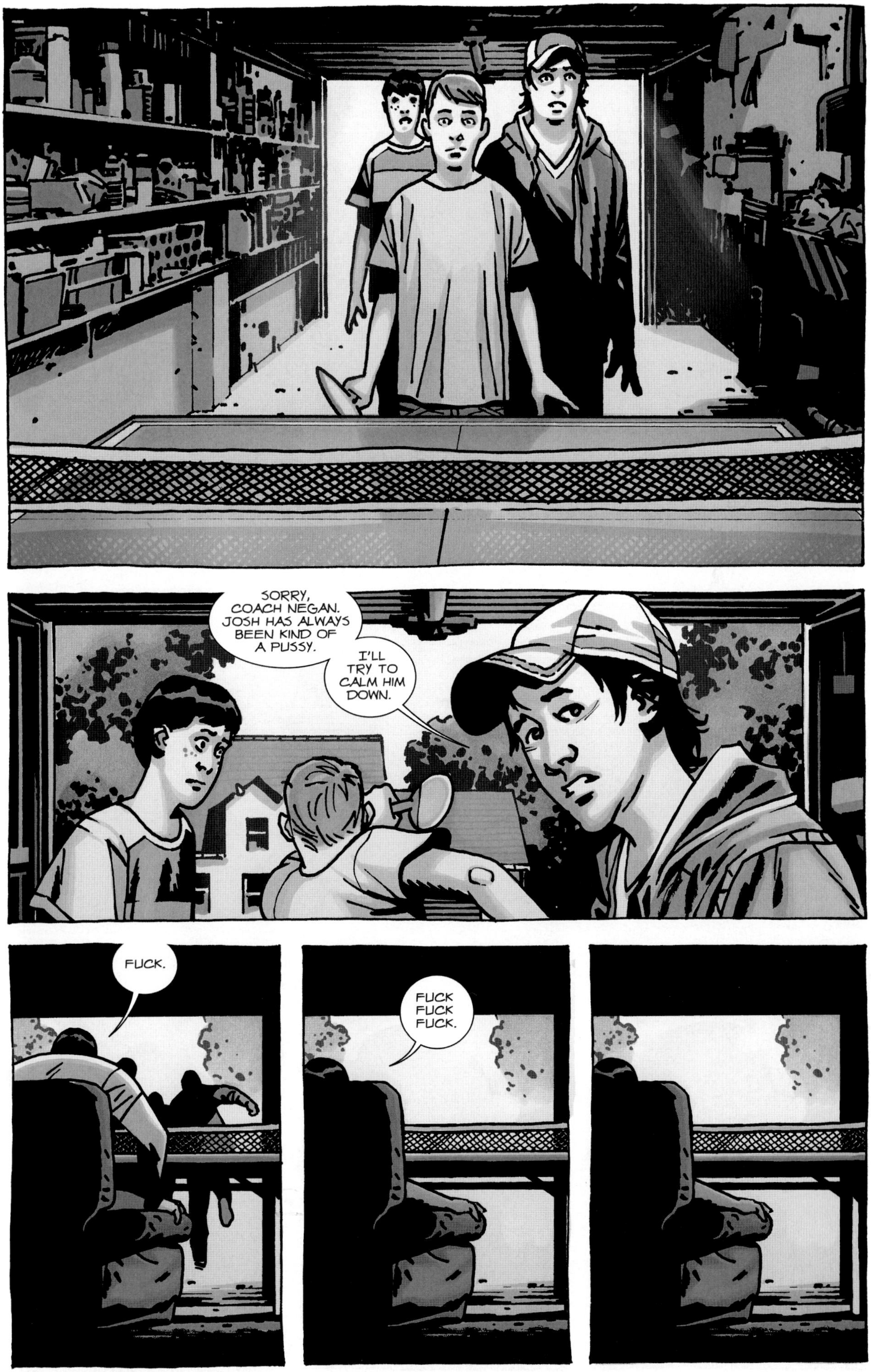
SORRY, COACH NEGAN. JOSH HAS ALWAYS BEEN KIND OF A PUSSY.
I'LL TRY TO CALM HIM DOWN.
FUCK.
FUCK FUCK FUCK.

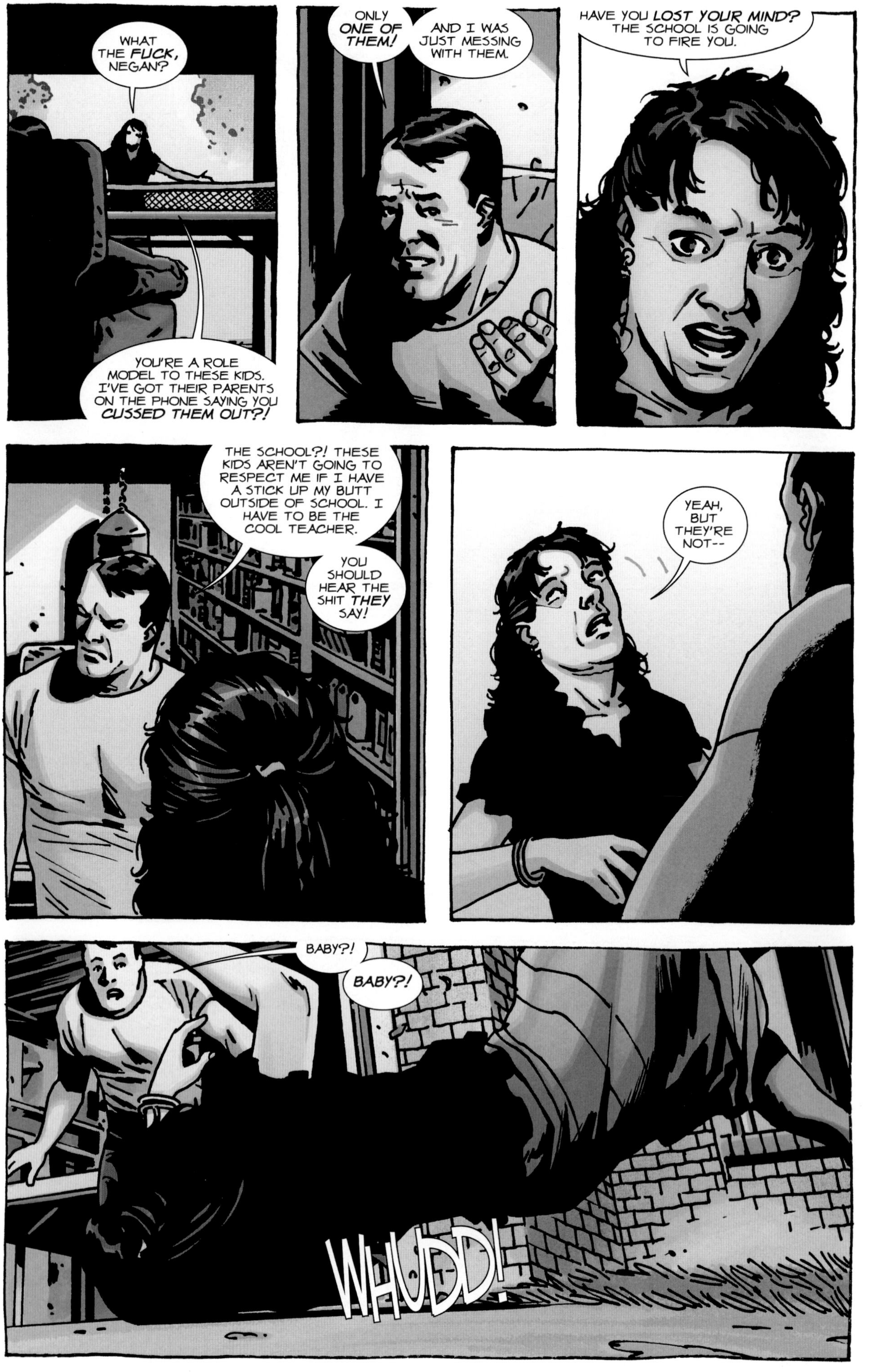
WHAT THE FUCK, NEGAN?
YOU'RE A ROLE MODEL TO THESE KIDS. I'VE GOT THEIR PARENTS ON THE PHONE SAYING YOU CUSSED THEM OUT?!
ONLY ONE OF THEM!
AND I WAS JUST MESSING WITH THEM.
HAVE YOU LOST YOUR MIND? THE SCHOOL IS GOING TO FIRE YOU.
THE SCHOOL?! THESE KIDS AREN'T GOING TO RESPECT ME IF I HAVE A STICK UP MY BUTT OUTSIDE OF SCHOOL. I HAVE TO BE THE COOL TEACHER.
YOU SHOULD HEAR THE SHIT THEY SAY!
YEAH, BUT THEY'RE NOT--
BABY?!
BABY?!
WHUDD!

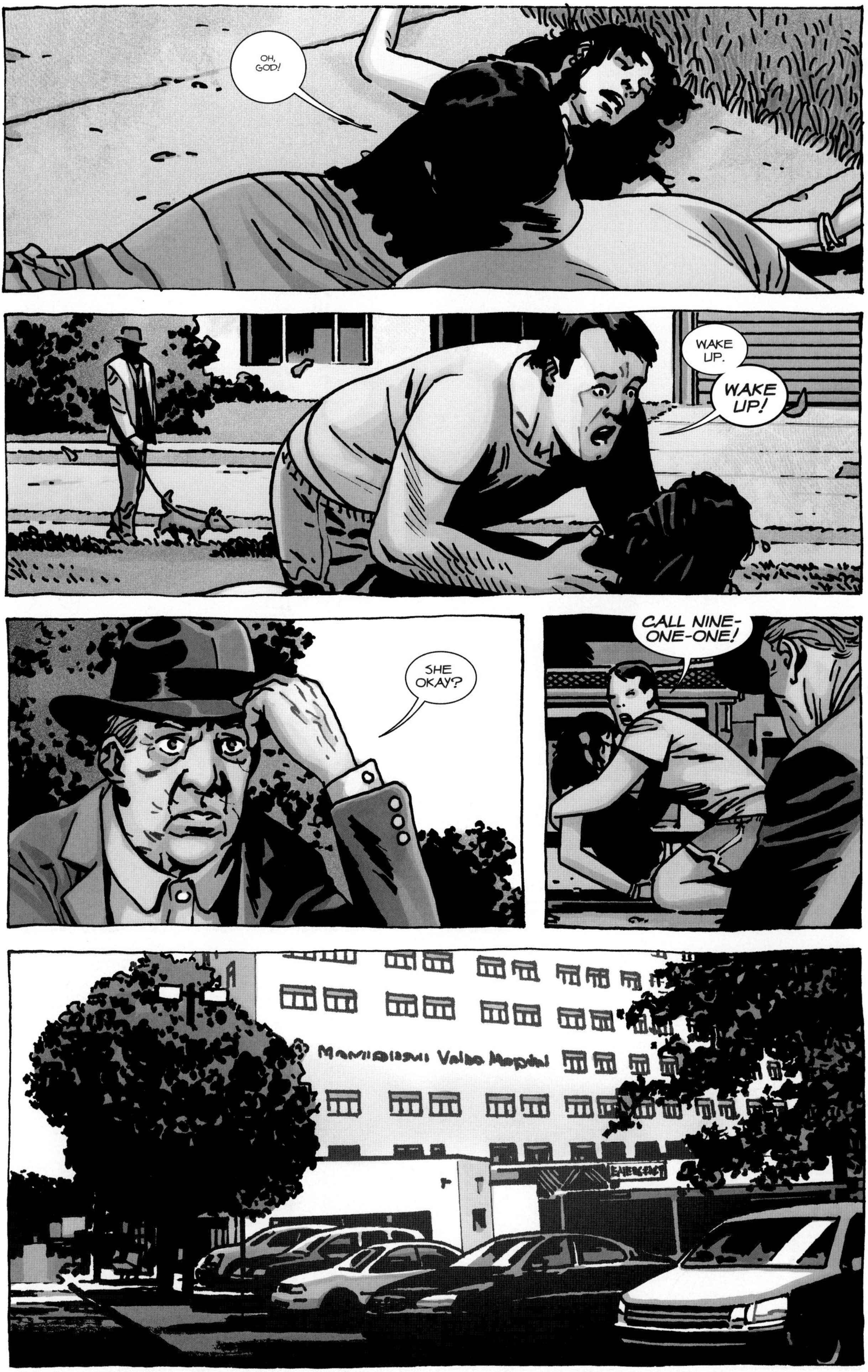
OH, GOD!
WAKE UP.
WAKE UP!
SHE OKAY?
CALL NINE-ONE-ONE!

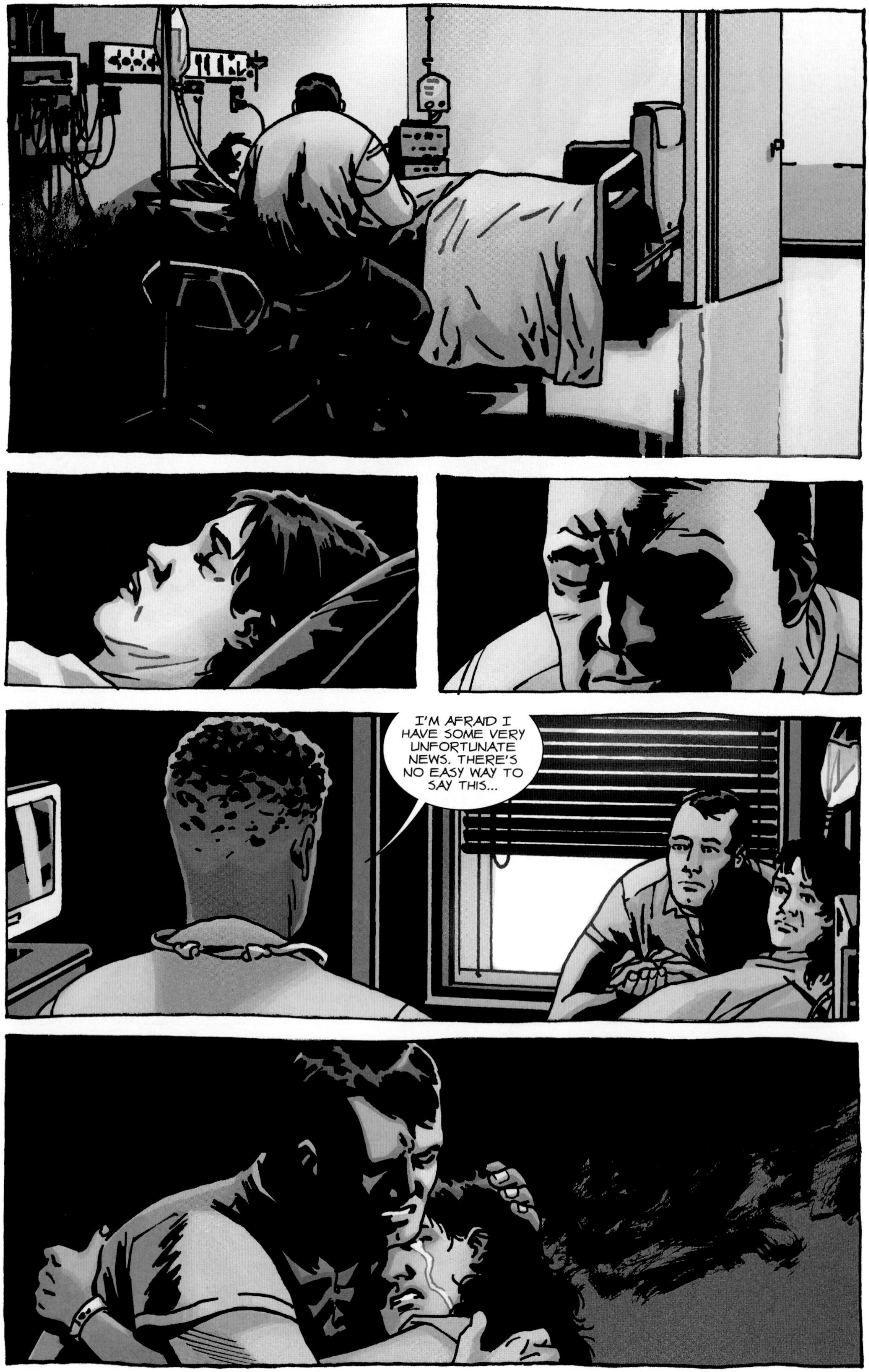
I'M AFRAID I HAVE SOME VERY UNFORTUNATE NEWS. THERE'S NO EASY WAY TO SAY THIS...

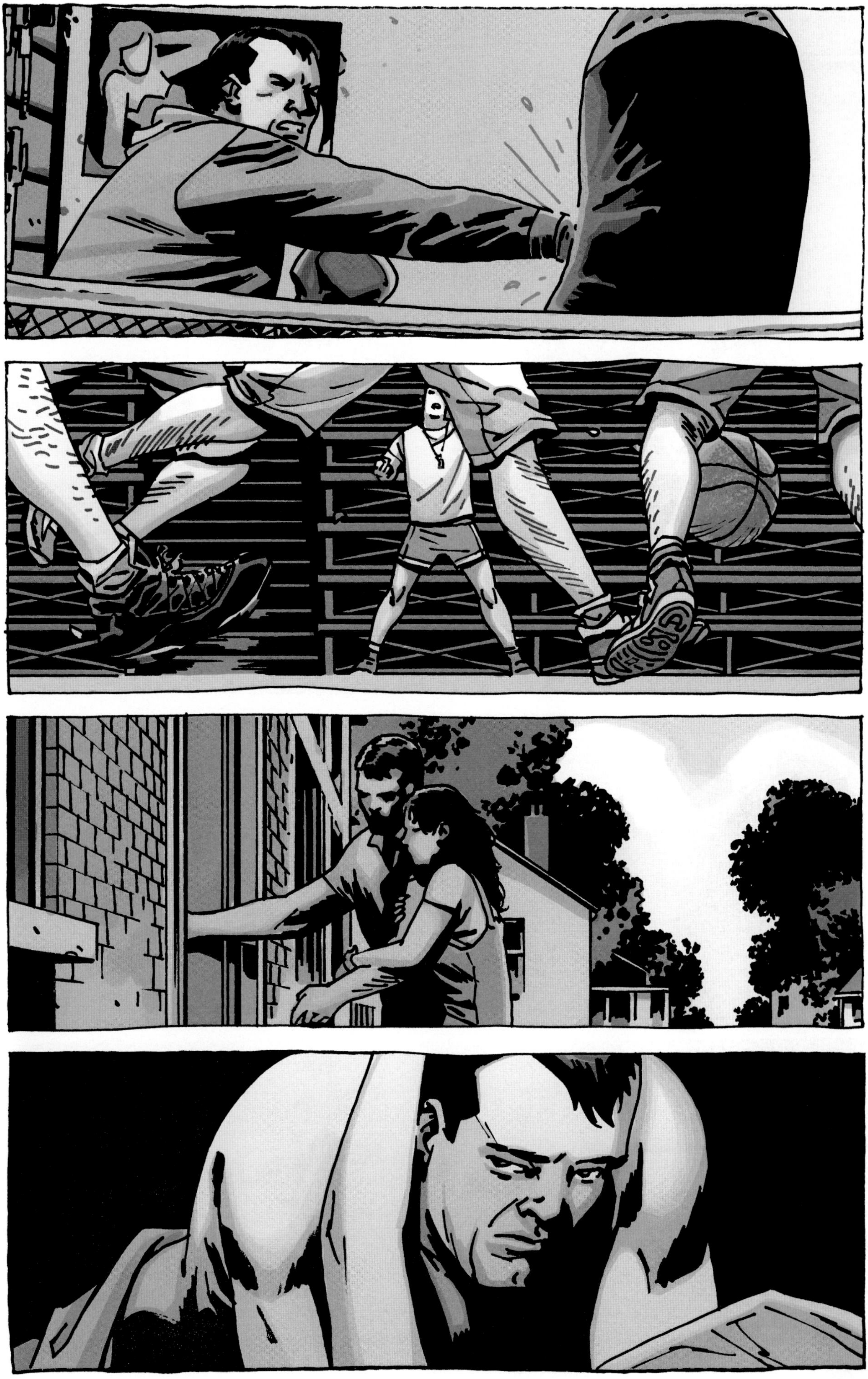

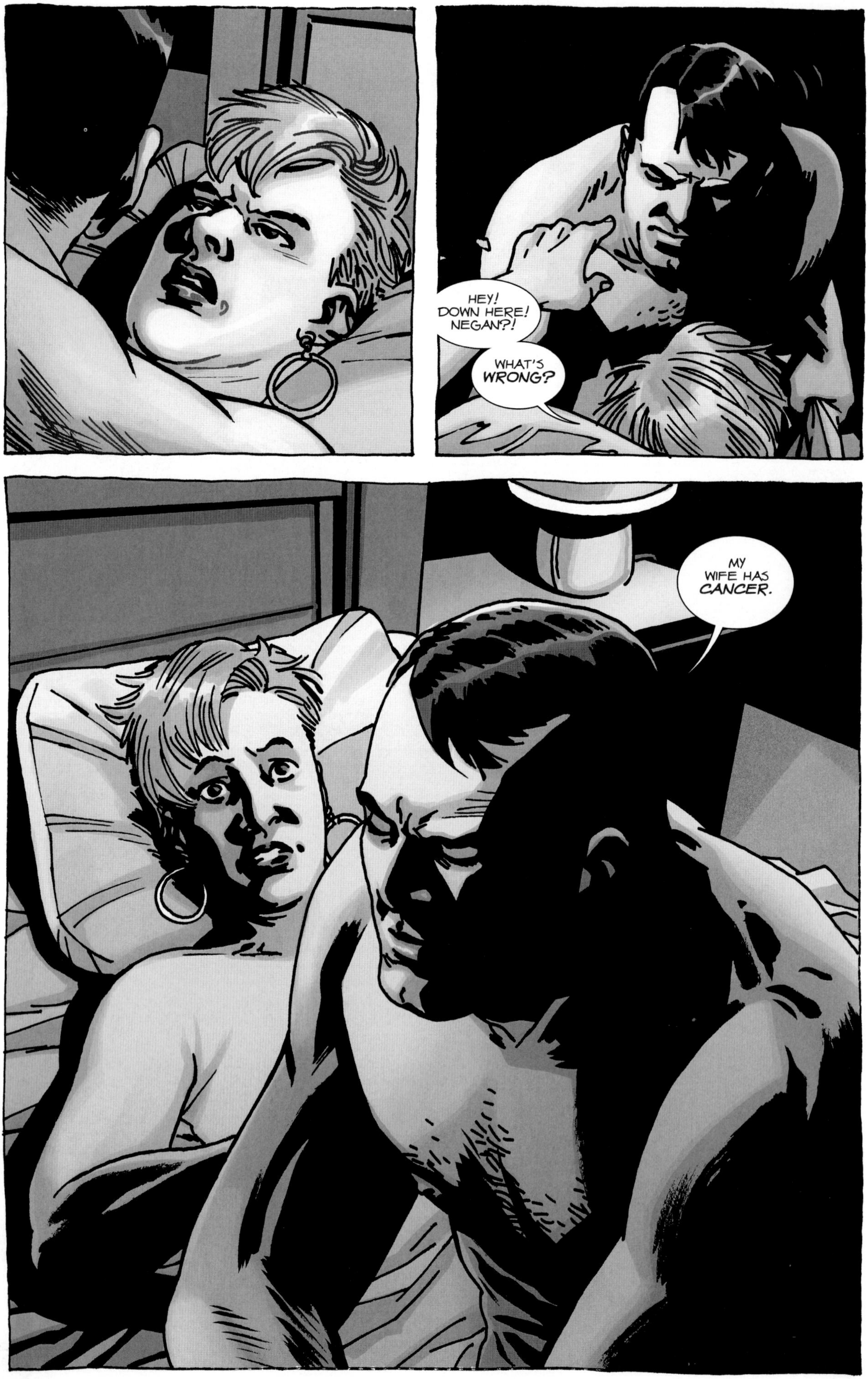
HEY! DOWN HERE! NEGAN?!
WHAT'S WRONG?
MY WIFE HAS CANCER.

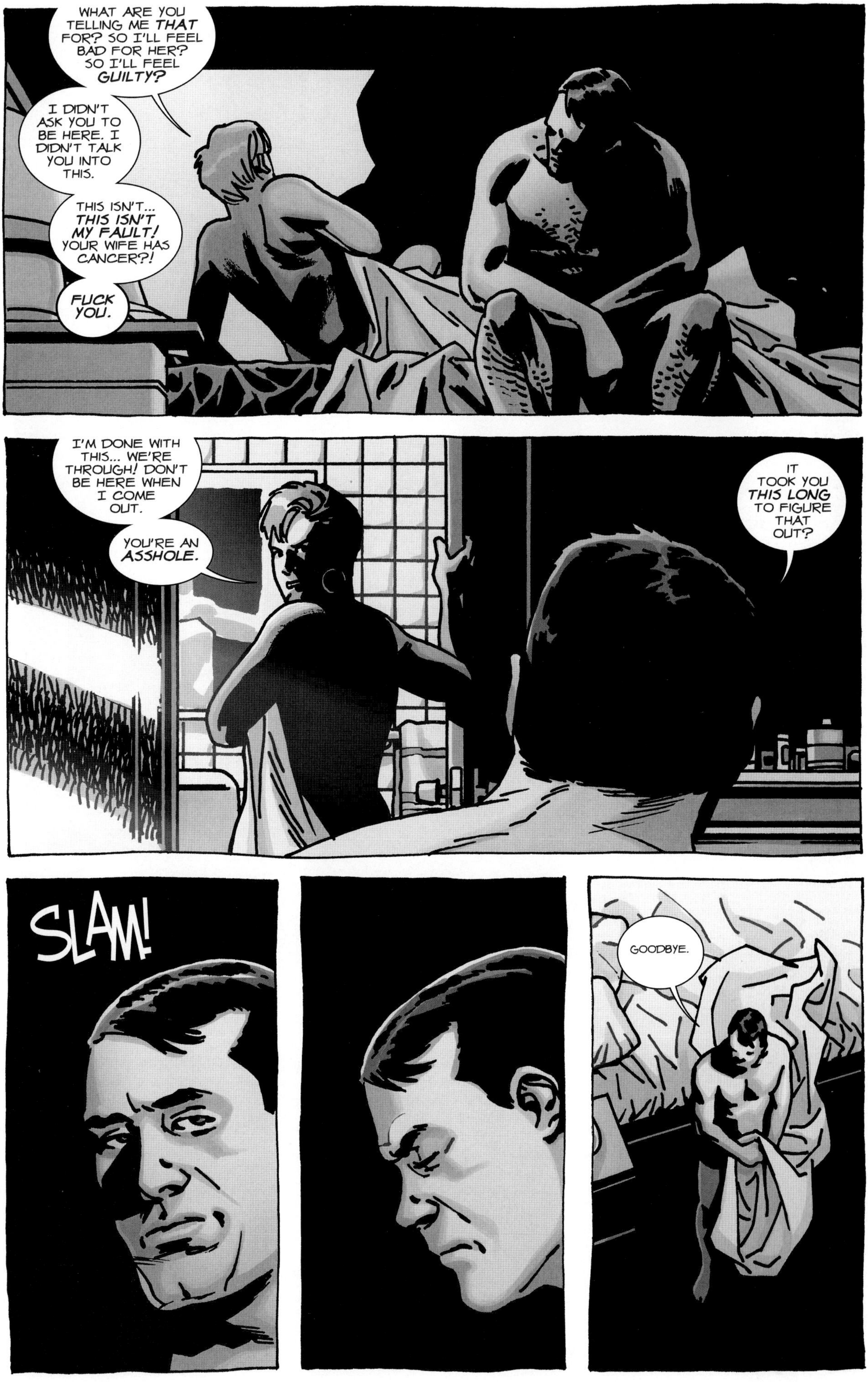
WHAT ARE YOU TELLING ME THAT FOR? SO I'LL FEEL BAD FOR HER? SO I'LL FEEL GUILTY?
I DIDN'T ASK YOU TO BE HERE. I DIDN'T TALK YOU INTO THIS.
THIS ISN'T... THIS ISN'T MY FAULT! YOUR WIFE HAS CANCER?!
FUCK YOU.
I'M DONE WITH THIS... WE'RE THROUGH! DON'T BE HERE WHEN I COME OUT.
YOU'RE AN ASSHOLE.
IT TOOK YOU THIS LONG TO FIGURE THAT OUT?
SLAM!
GOODBYE.

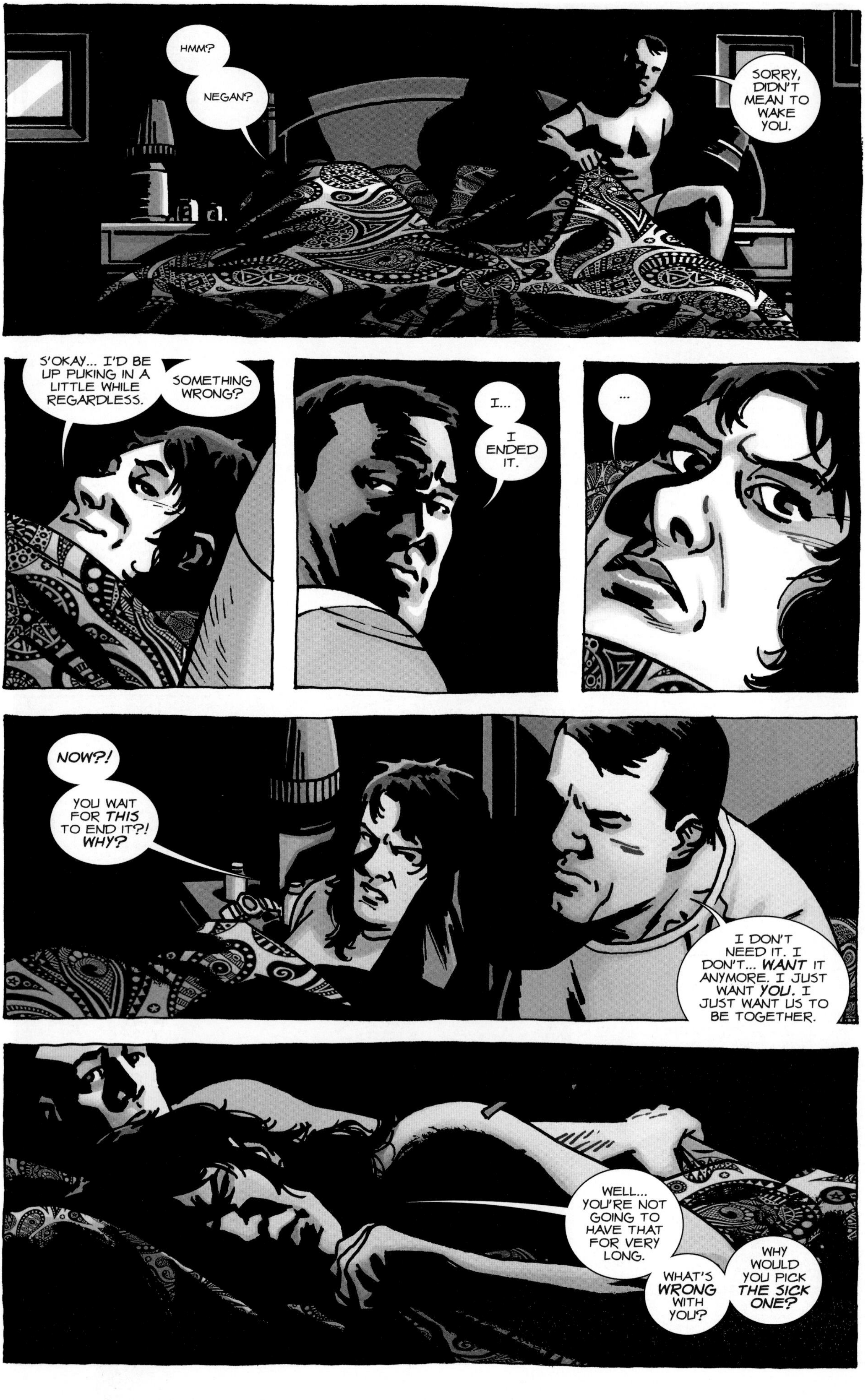
HMM?
NEGAN?
SORRY, DIDN'T MEAN TO WAKE YOU.
S'OKAY... I'D BE UP PUKING IN A LITTLE WHILE REGARDLESS.
SOMETHING WRONG?
I...
I ENDED IT.
...
NOW?!
YOU WAIT FOR THIS TO END IT?! WHY?
I DON'T NEED IT. I DON'T... WANT IT ANYMORE. I JUST WANT YOU. I JUST WANT US TO BE TOGETHER.
WELL... YOU'RE NOT GOING TO HAVE THAT FOR VERY LONG.
WHAT'S WRONG WITH YOU?
WHY WOULD YOU PICK THE SICK ONE?

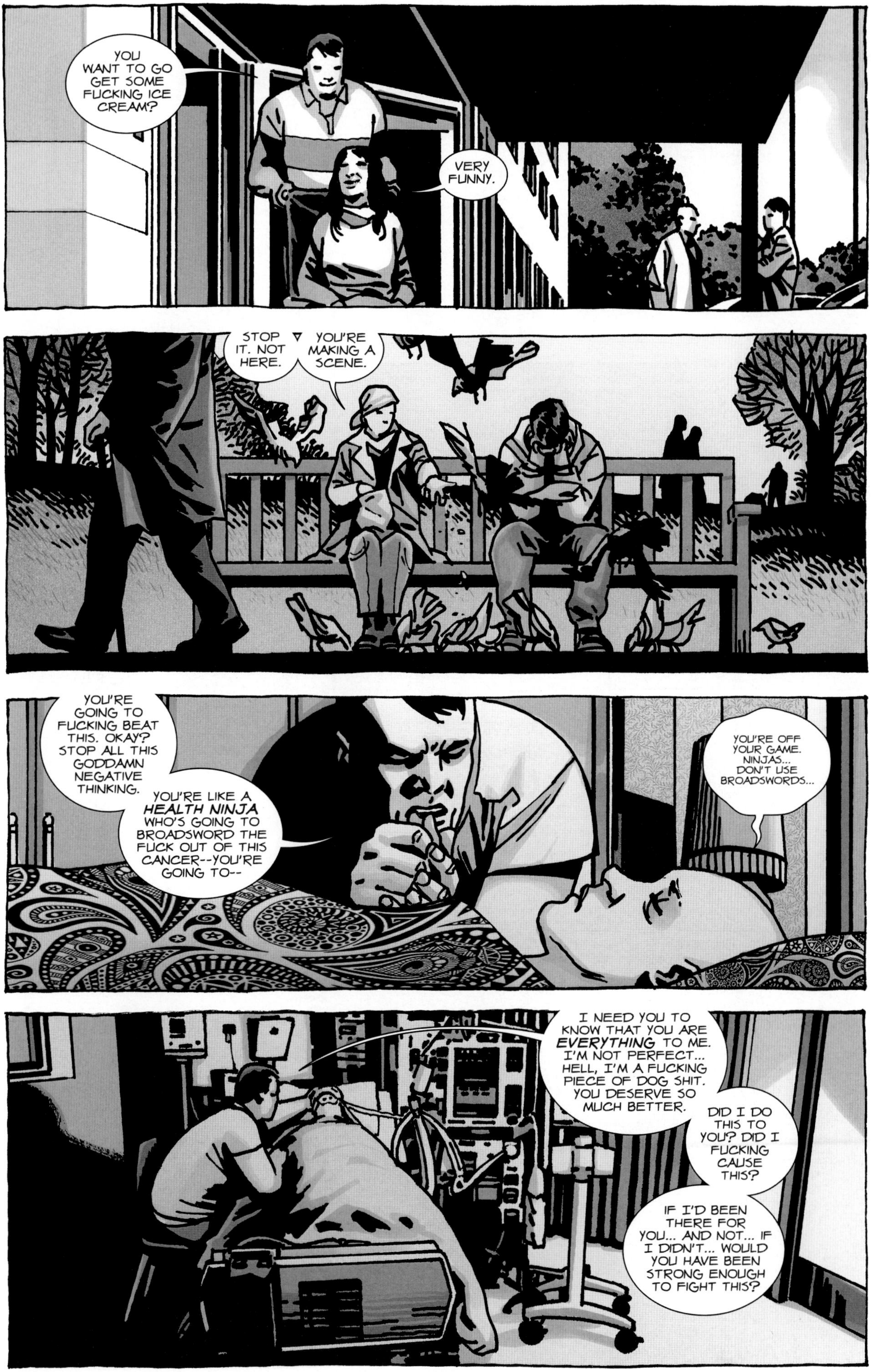
YOU WANT TO GO GET SOME FUCKING ICE CREAM?
VERY FUNNY.
STOP IT. NOT HERE.
YOU'RE MAKING A SCENE.
YOU'RE GOING TO FUCKING BEAT THIS. OKAY? STOP ALL THIS GODDAMN NEGATIVE THINKING.
YOU'RE LIKE A *HEALTH NINJA* WHO'S GOING TO BROADSWORD THE FUCK OUT OF THIS CANCER--YOU'RE GOING TO--
YOU'RE OFF YOUR GAME. NINJAS... DON'T USE BROADSWORDS...
I NEED YOU TO KNOW THAT YOU ARE *EVERYTHING* TO ME. I'M NOT PERFECT... HELL, I'M A FUCKING PIECE OF DOG SHIT. YOU DESERVE SO MUCH BETTER.
DID I DO THIS TO YOU? DID I FUCKING CAUSE THIS?
IF I'D BEEN THERE FOR YOU... AND NOT... IF I DIDN'T... WOULD YOU HAVE BEEN STRONG ENOUGH TO FIGHT THIS?

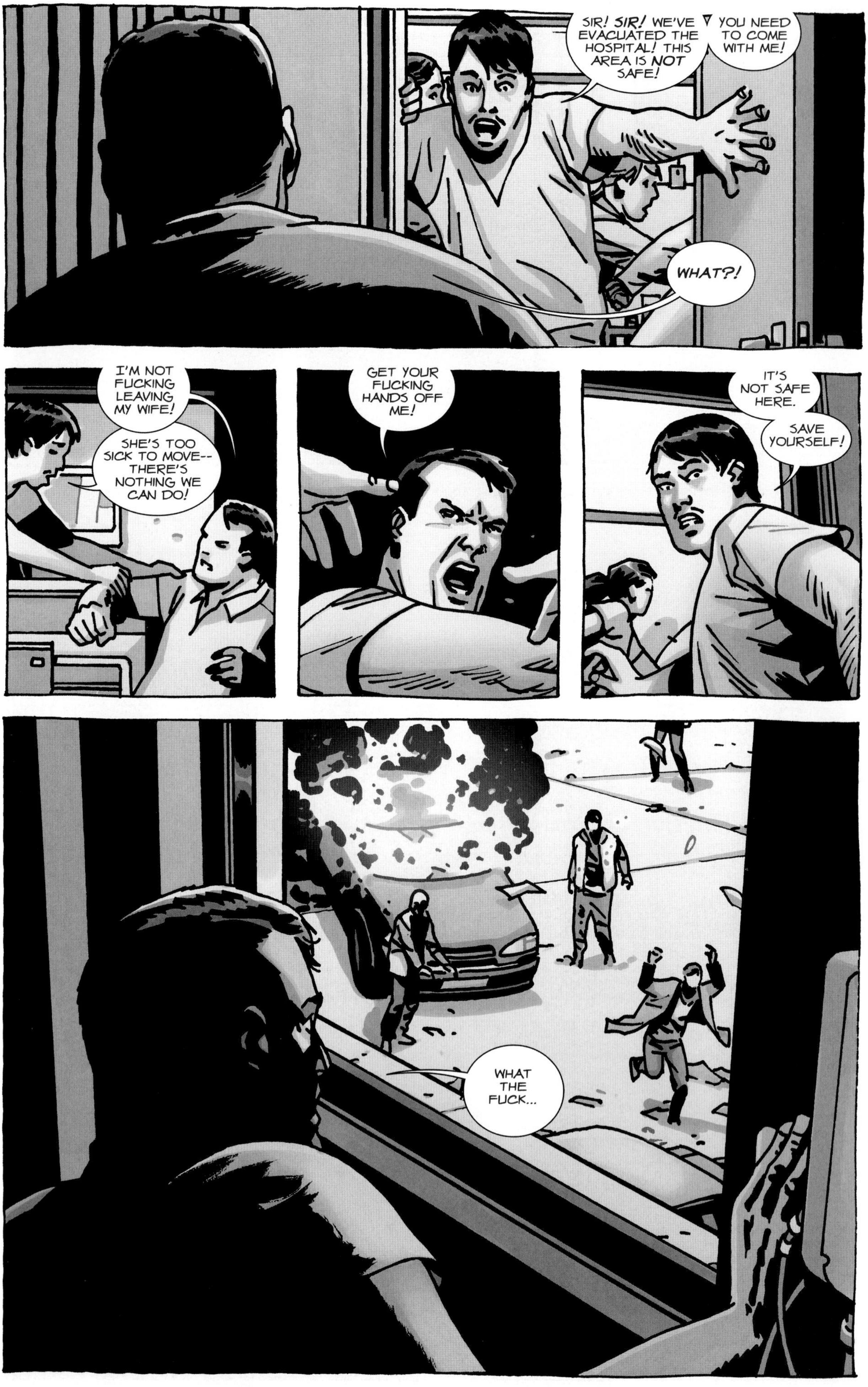
SIR! SIR! WE'VE EVACUATED THE HOSPITAL! THIS AREA IS NOT SAFE!
YOU NEED TO COME WITH ME!
WHAT?!
I'M NOT FUCKING LEAVING MY WIFE!
SHE'S TOO SICK TO MOVE-- THERE'S NOTHING WE CAN DO!
GET YOUR FUCKING HANDS OFF ME!
IT'S NOT SAFE HERE.
SAVE YOURSELF!
WHAT THE FUCK...

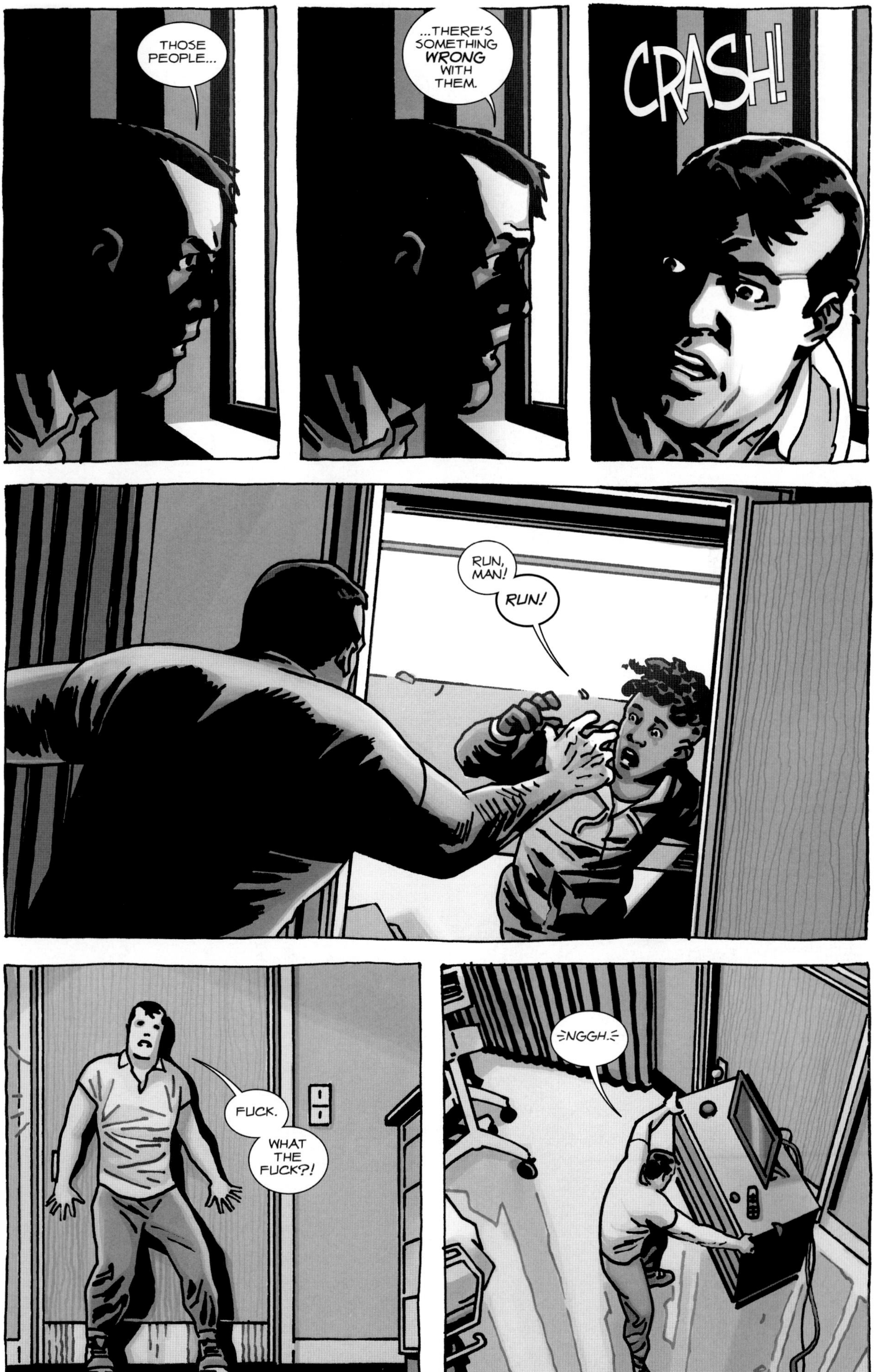
THOSE PEOPLE...
...THERE'S SOMETHING WRONG WITH THEM.
CRASH!
RUN, MAN!
RUN!
FUCK.
WHAT THE FUCK?!
NGGH.

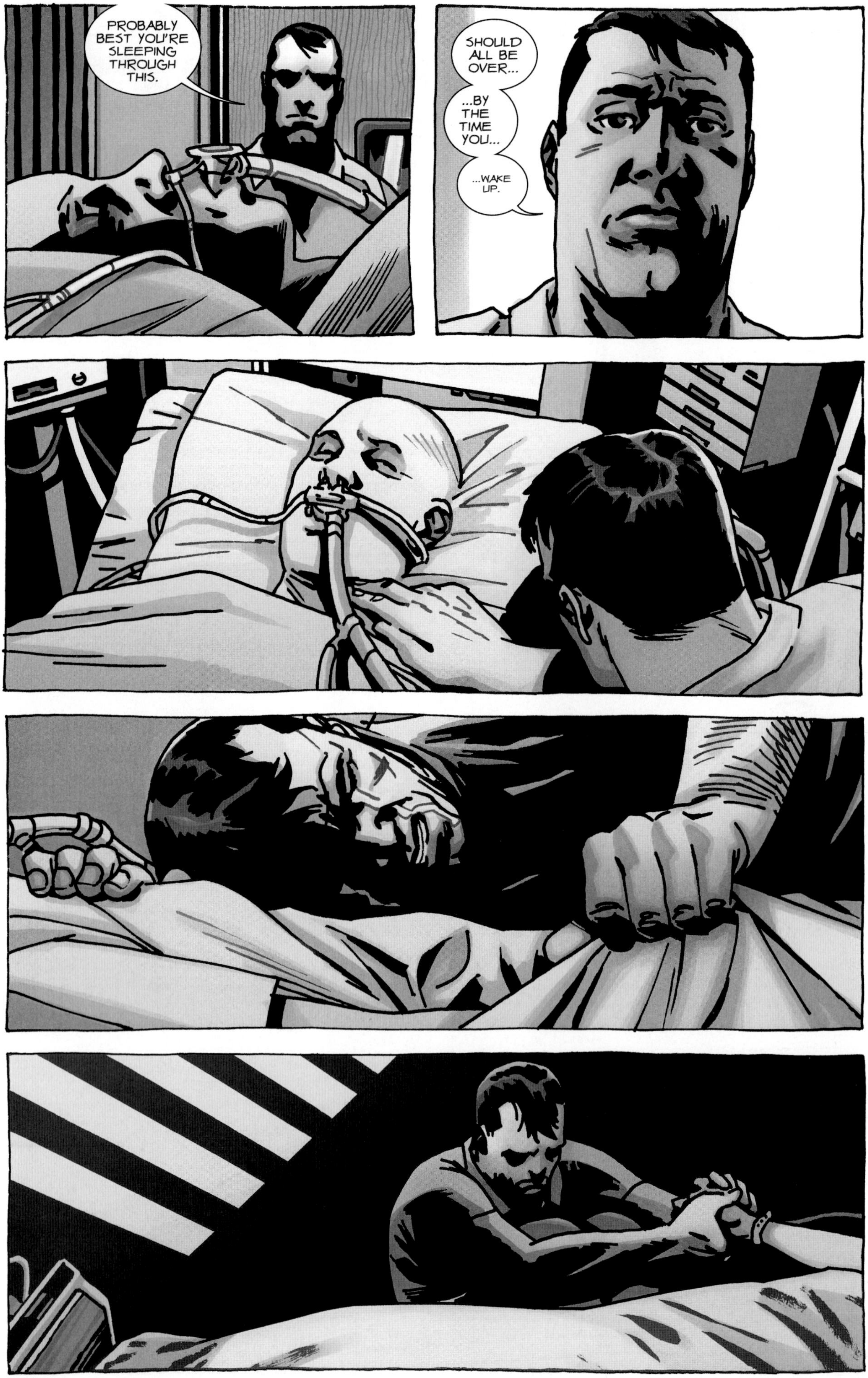
PROBABLY BEST YOU'RE SLEEPING THROUGH THIS.
SHOULD ALL BE OVER...
...BY THE TIME YOU...
...WAKE UP.

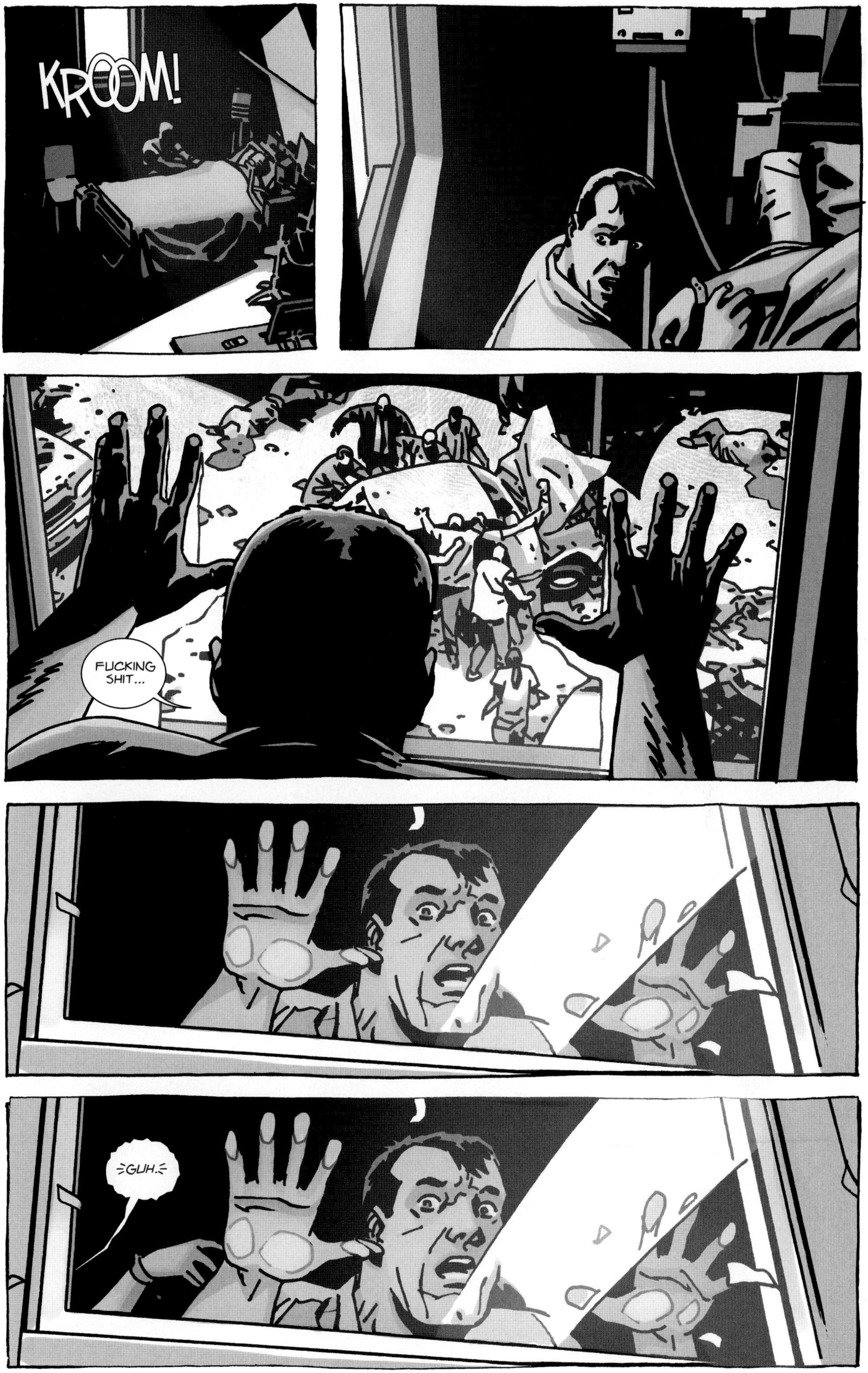
KROOM!
FUCKING SHIT...
GUH.

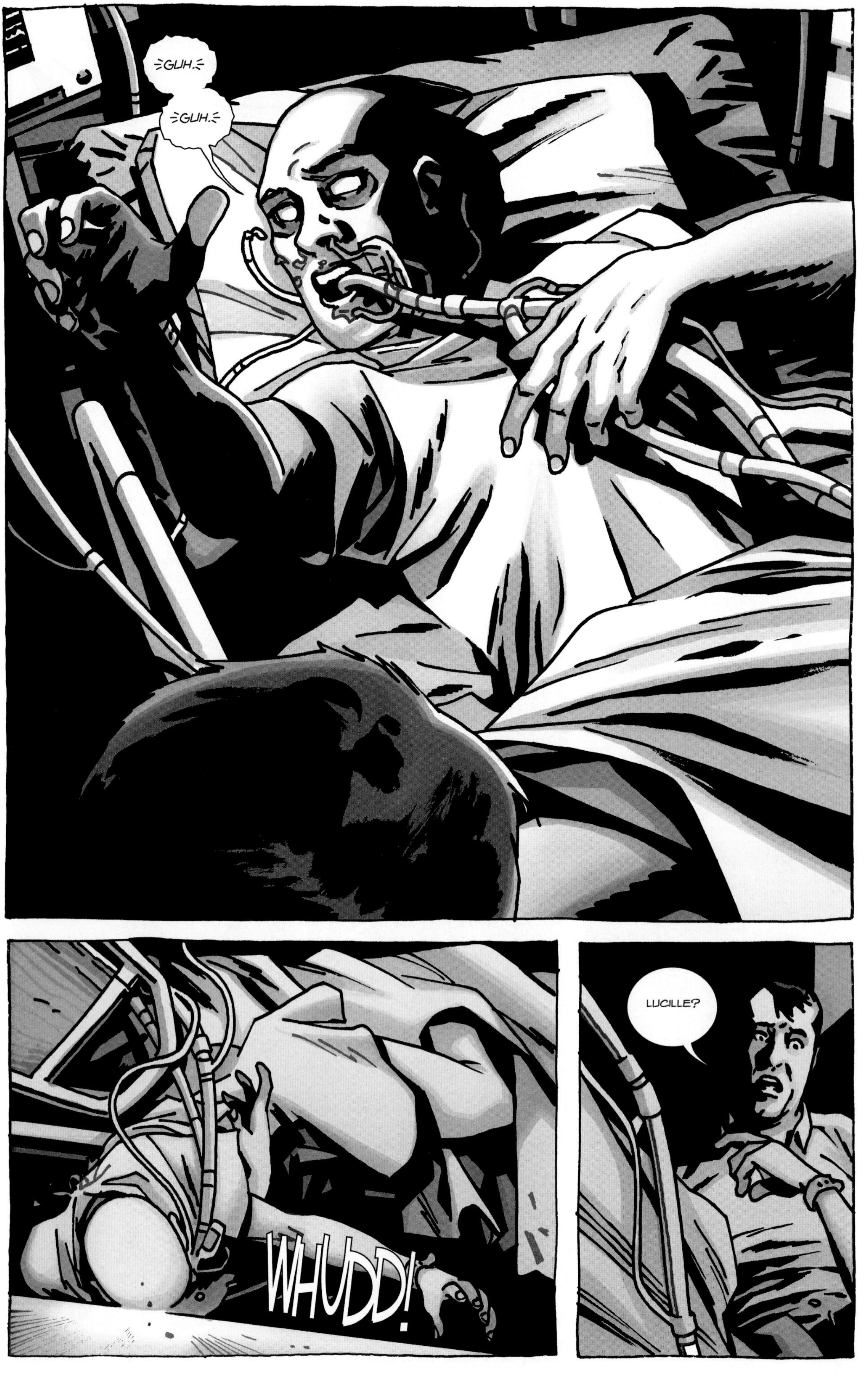
GUH.
GUH.
WHUDD!
LUCILLE?

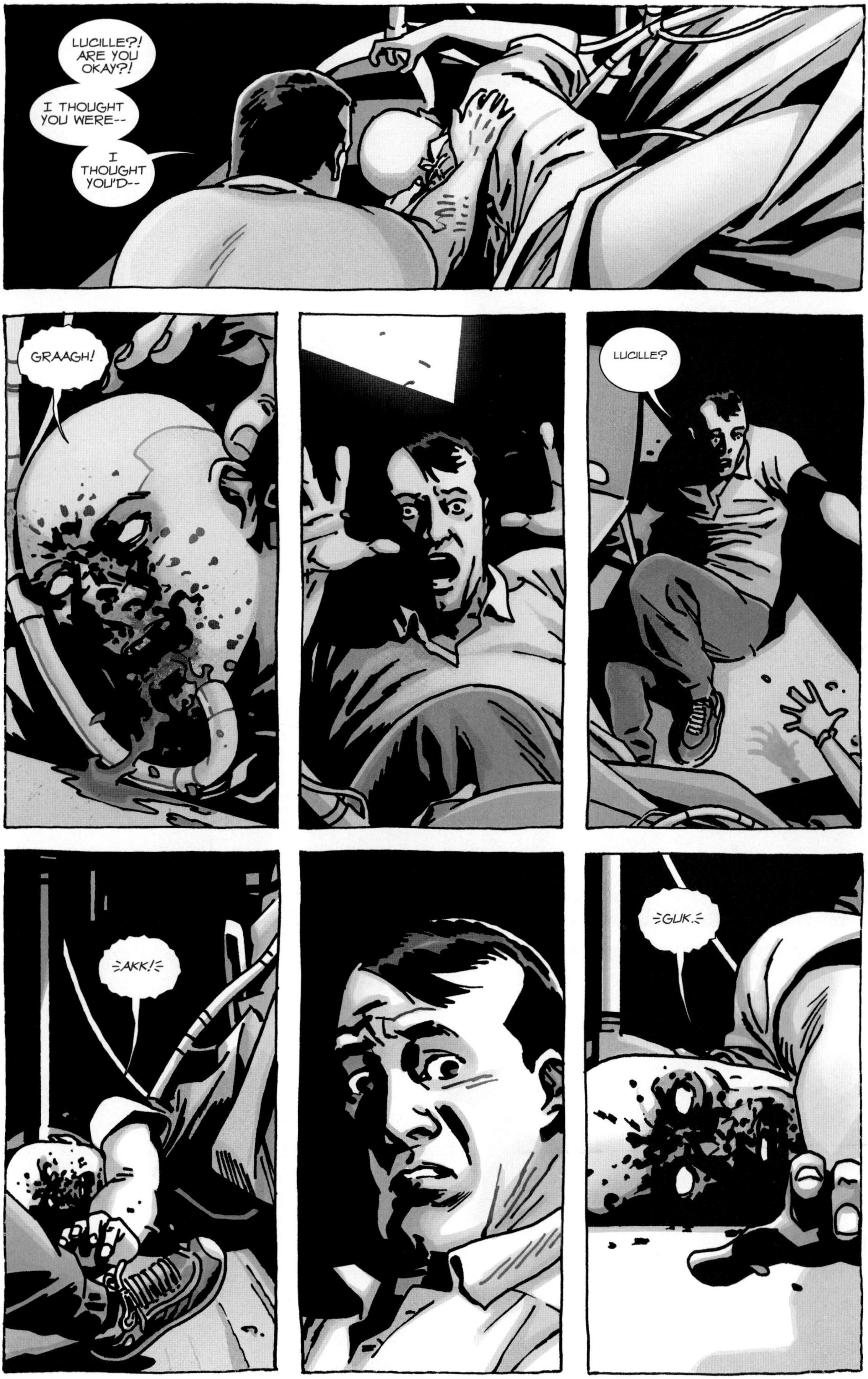
LUCILLE?! ARE YOU OKAY?!
I THOUGHT YOU WERE--
I THOUGHT YOU'D--
GRAAGH!
LUCILLE?
AKK!
GUK.

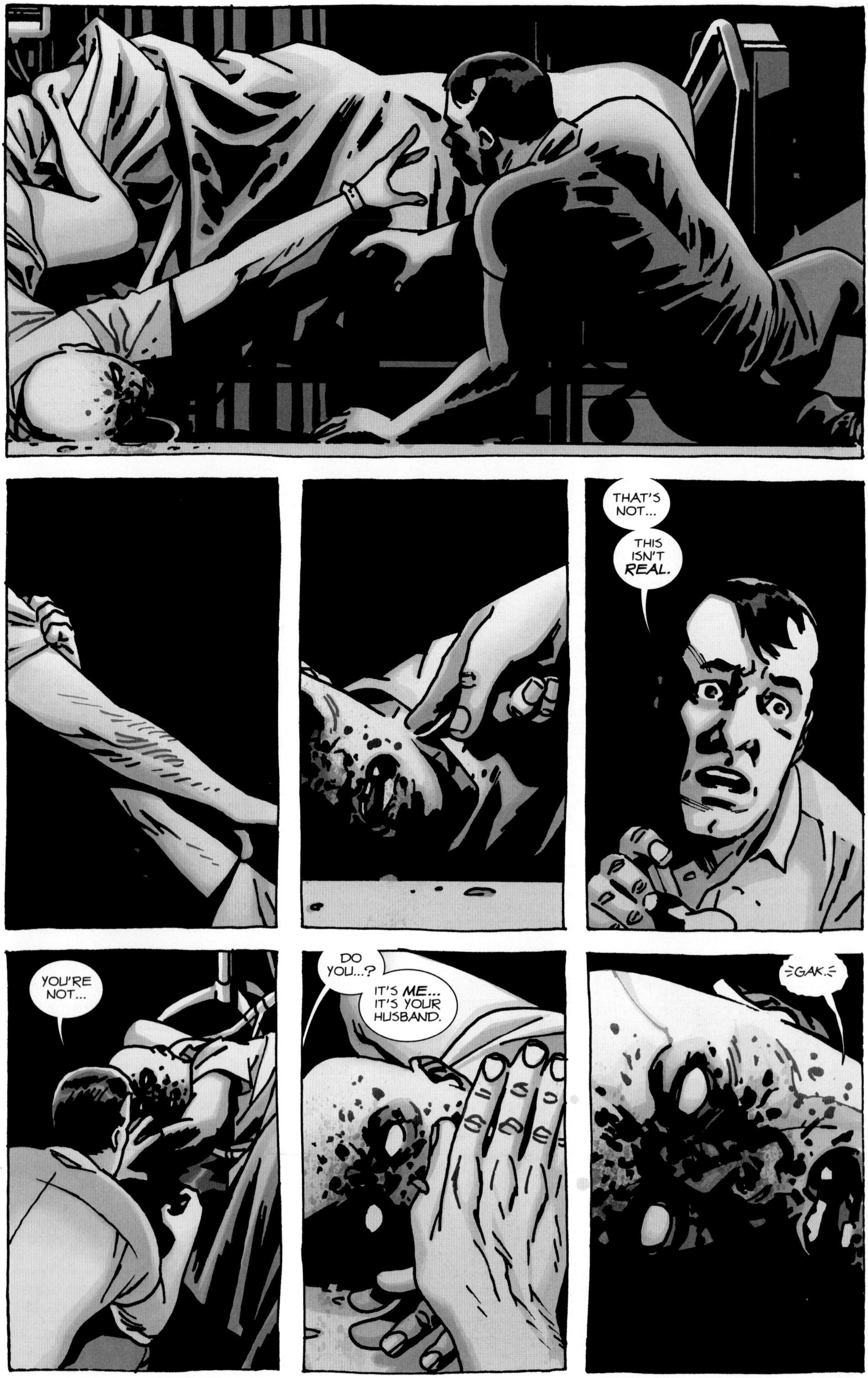
THAT'S NOT...
THIS ISN'T REAL.
YOU'RE NOT...
DO YOU...?
IT'S ME... IT'S YOUR HUSBAND.
GAK.

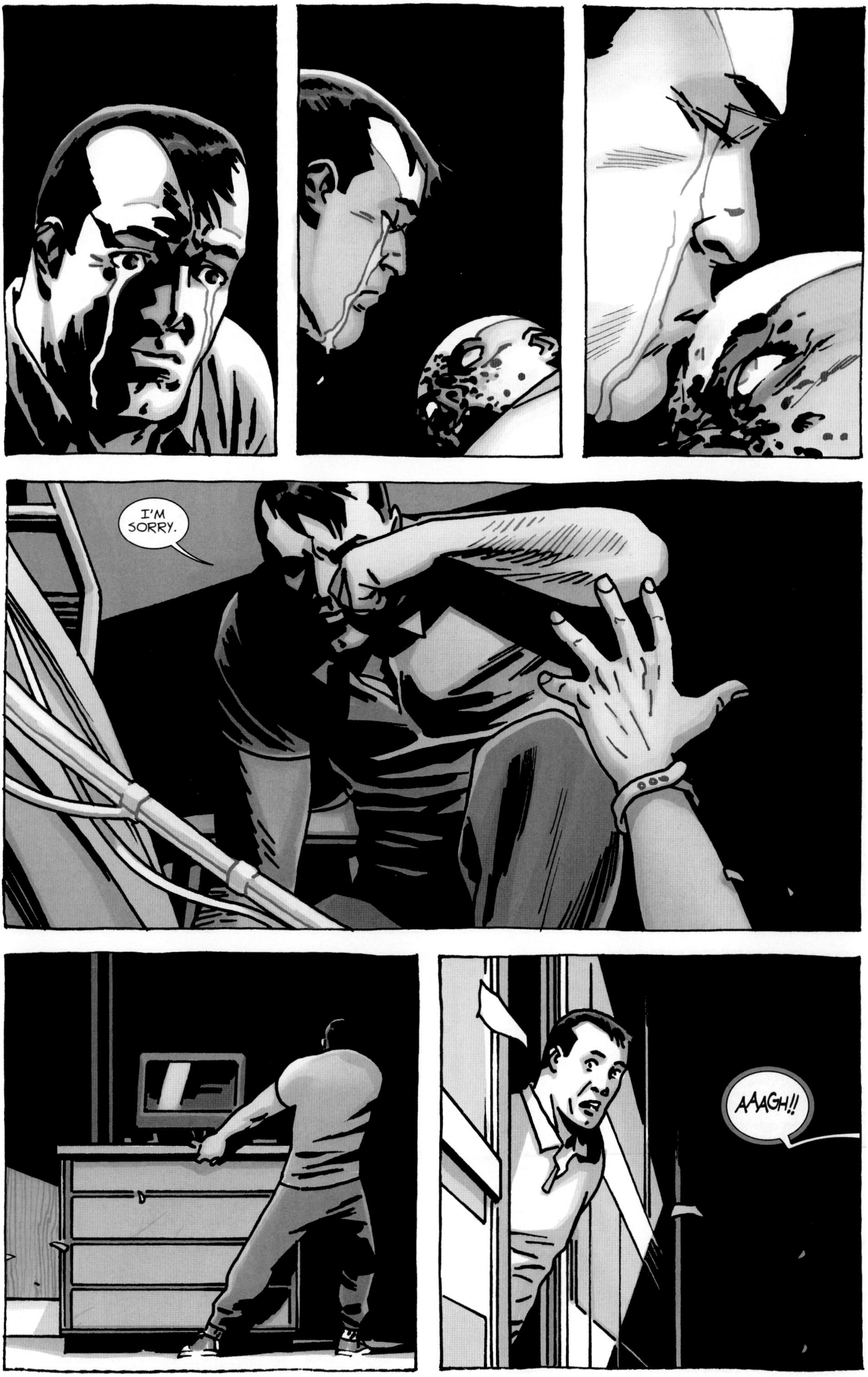
I'M SORRY.
AAAGH!!

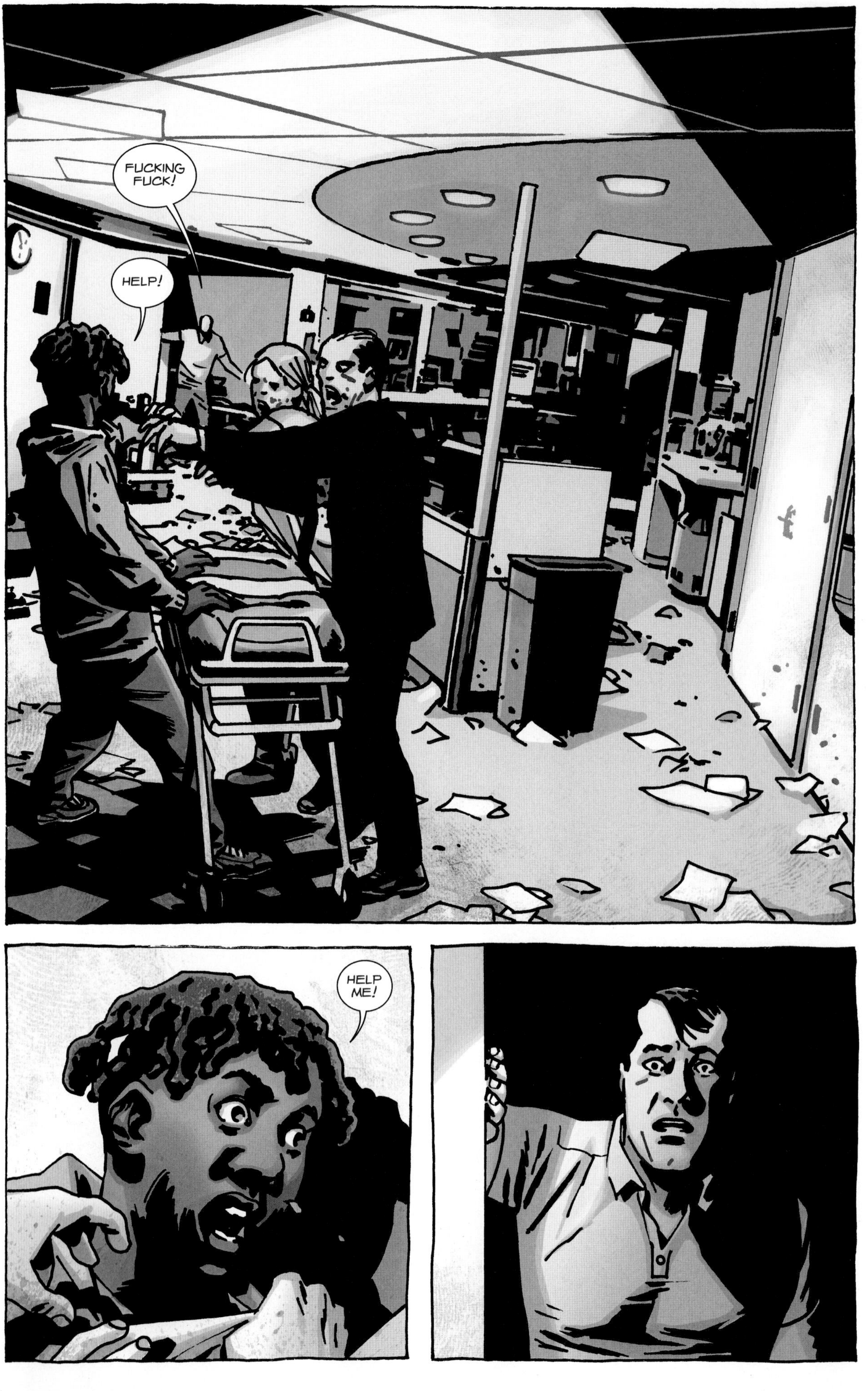
FUCKING FUCK!
HELP!
HELP ME!

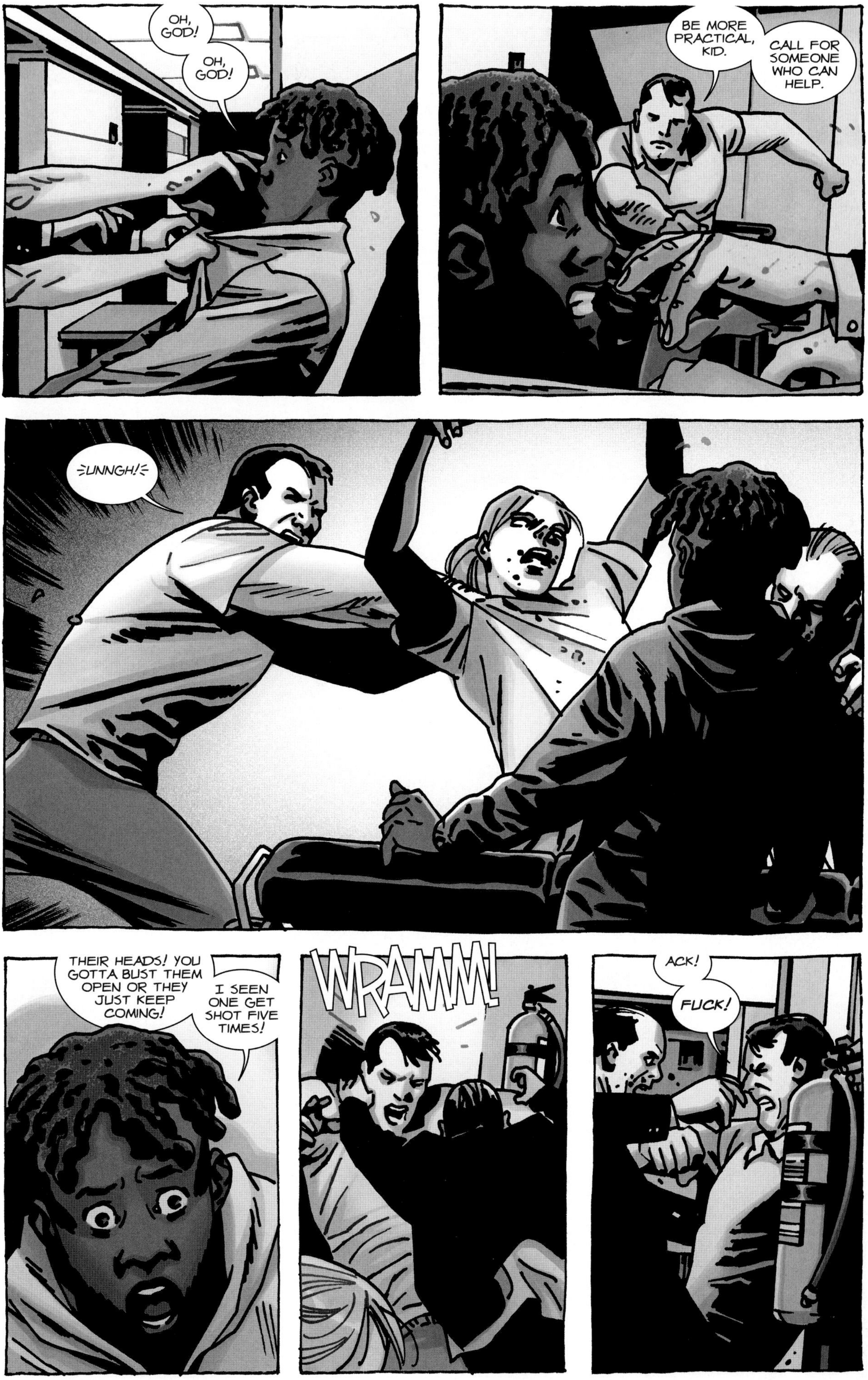
OH, GOD!
OH, GOD!
BE MORE PRACTICAL, KID.
CALL FOR SOMEONE WHO CAN HELP.
UNNGH!
THEIR HEADS! YOU GOTTA BUST THEM OPEN OR THEY JUST KEEP COMING!
I SEEN ONE GET SHOT FIVE TIMES!
WRAMM!
ACK!
FUCK!

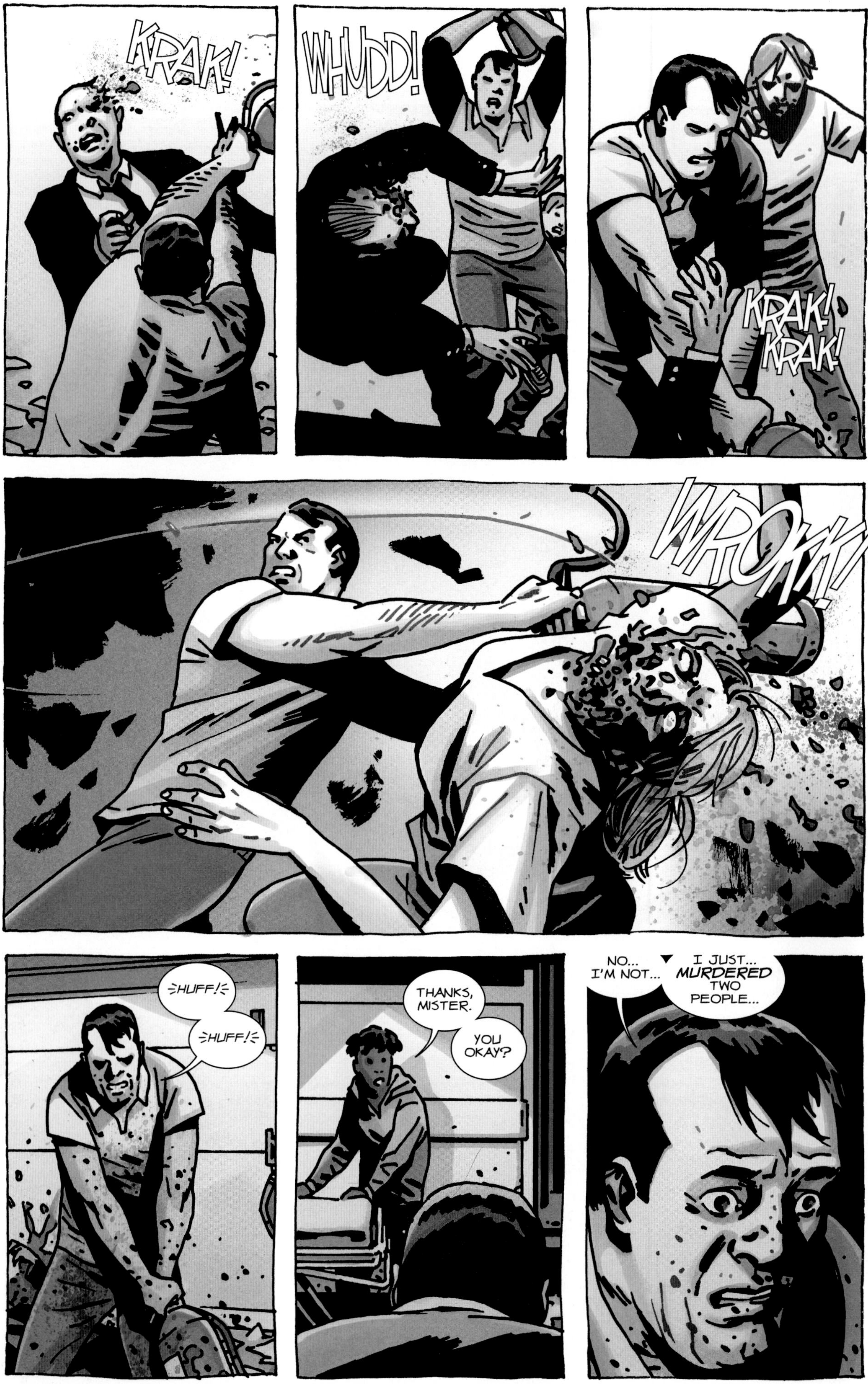
KRAK!
WHUDD!
KRAK! KRAK!
WROKK!
HUFF!
HUFF!
THANKS, MISTER.
YOU OKAY?
NO... I'M NOT...
I JUST... MURDERED TWO PEOPLE...

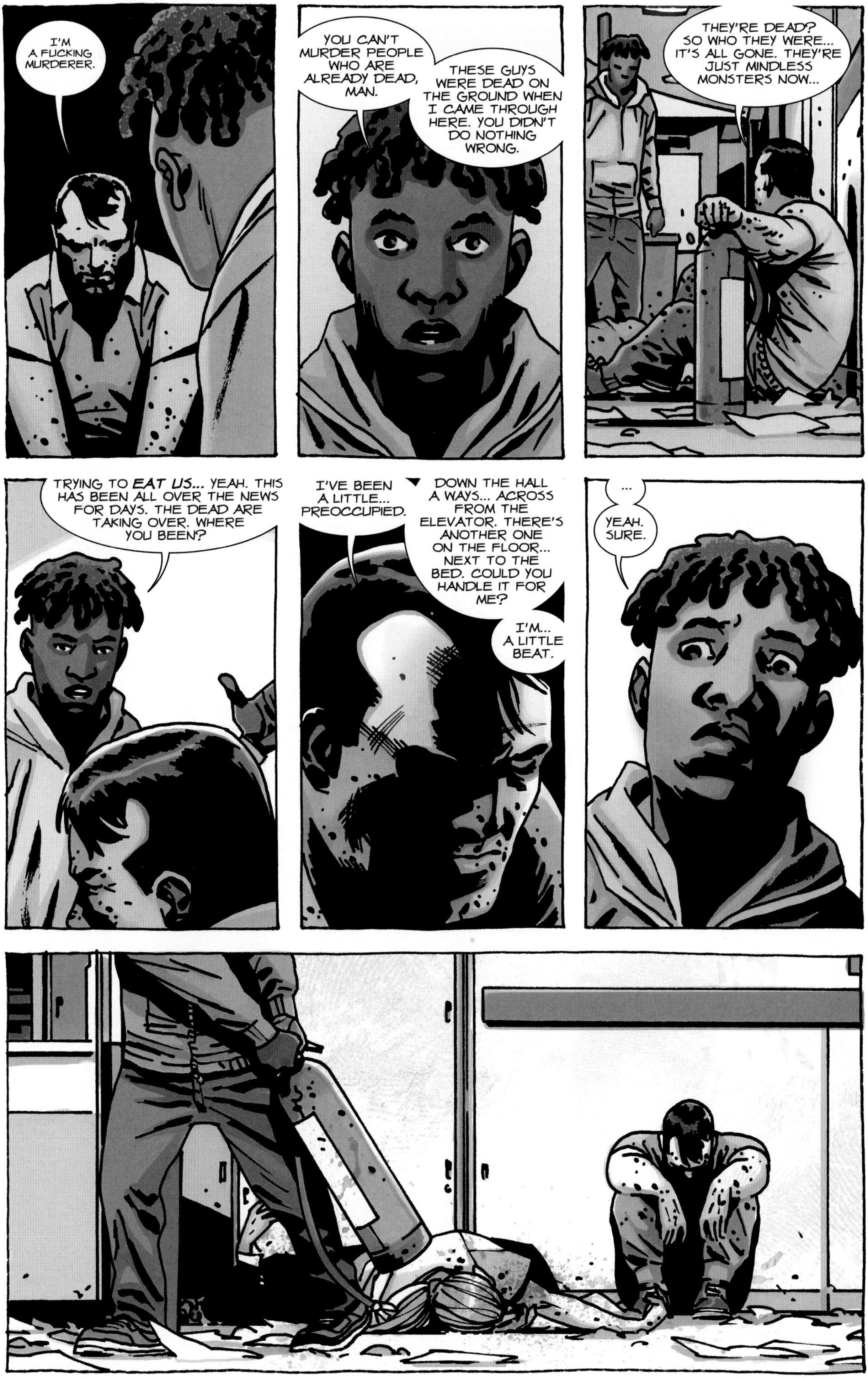
I'M A FUCKING MURDERER.
YOU CAN'T MURDER PEOPLE WHO ARE ALREADY DEAD, MAN.
THESE GUYS WERE DEAD ON THE GROUND WHEN I CAME THROUGH HERE. YOU DIDN'T DO NOTHING WRONG.
THEY'RE DEAD? SO WHO THEY WERE... IT'S ALL GONE. THEY'RE JUST MINDLESS MONSTERS NOW...
TRYING TO EAT US... YEAH. THIS HAS BEEN ALL OVER THE NEWS FOR DAYS. THE DEAD ARE TAKING OVER. WHERE YOU BEEN?
I'VE BEEN A LITTLE... PREOCCUPIED.
DOWN THE HALL A WAYS... ACROSS FROM THE ELEVATOR. THERE'S ANOTHER ONE ON THE FLOOR... NEXT TO THE BED. COULD YOU HANDLE IT FOR ME?
I'M... A LITTLE BEAT.
...
YEAH. SURE.

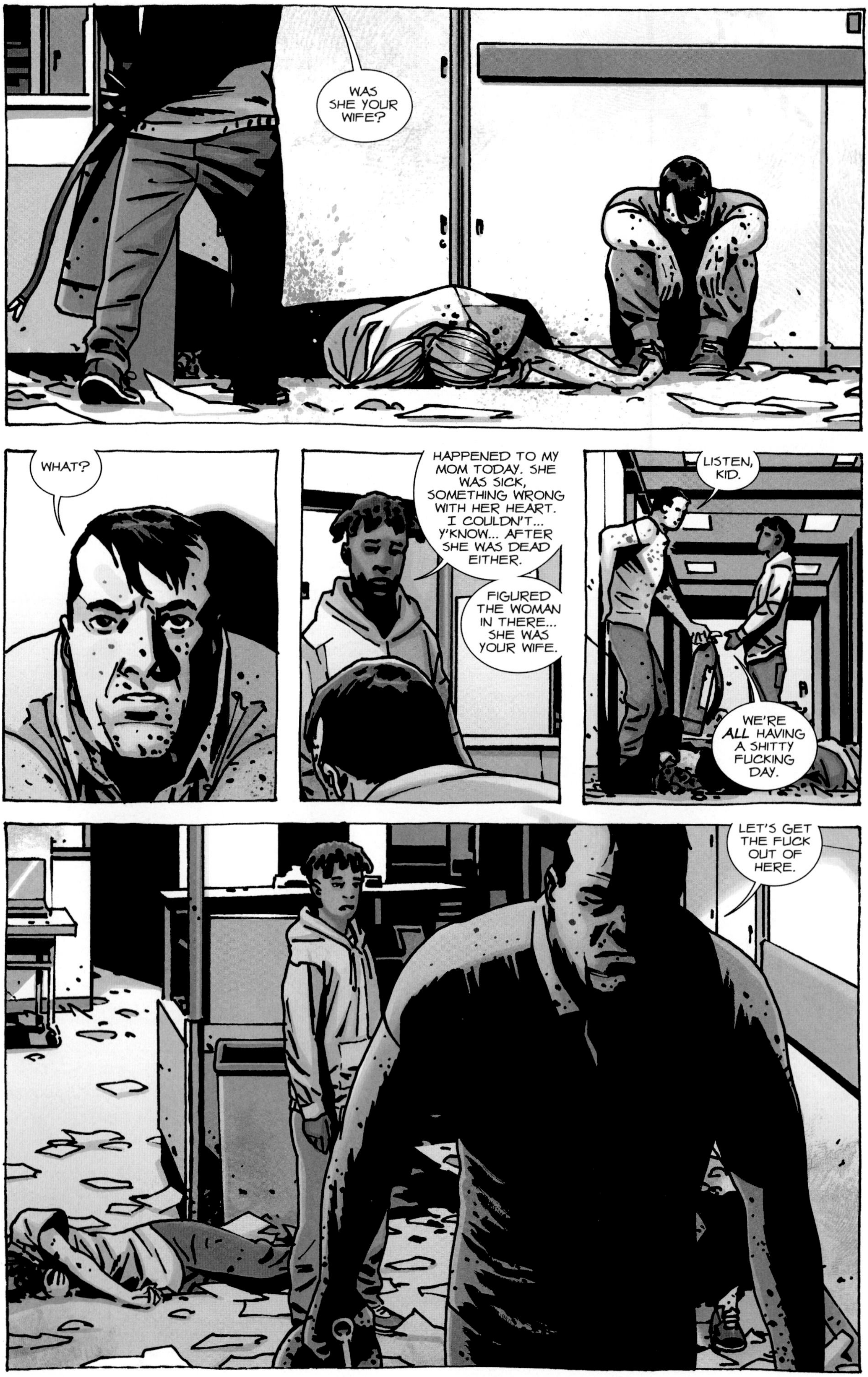
WAS SHE YOUR WIFE?
WHAT?
HAPPENED TO MY MOM TODAY. SHE WAS SICK, SOMETHING WRONG WITH HER HEART. I COULDN'T... Y'KNOW... AFTER SHE WAS DEAD EITHER.
FIGURED THE WOMAN IN THERE... SHE WAS YOUR WIFE.
LISTEN, KID.
WE'RE *ALL* HAVING A SHITTY FUCKING DAY.
LET'S GET THE FUCK OUT OF HERE.

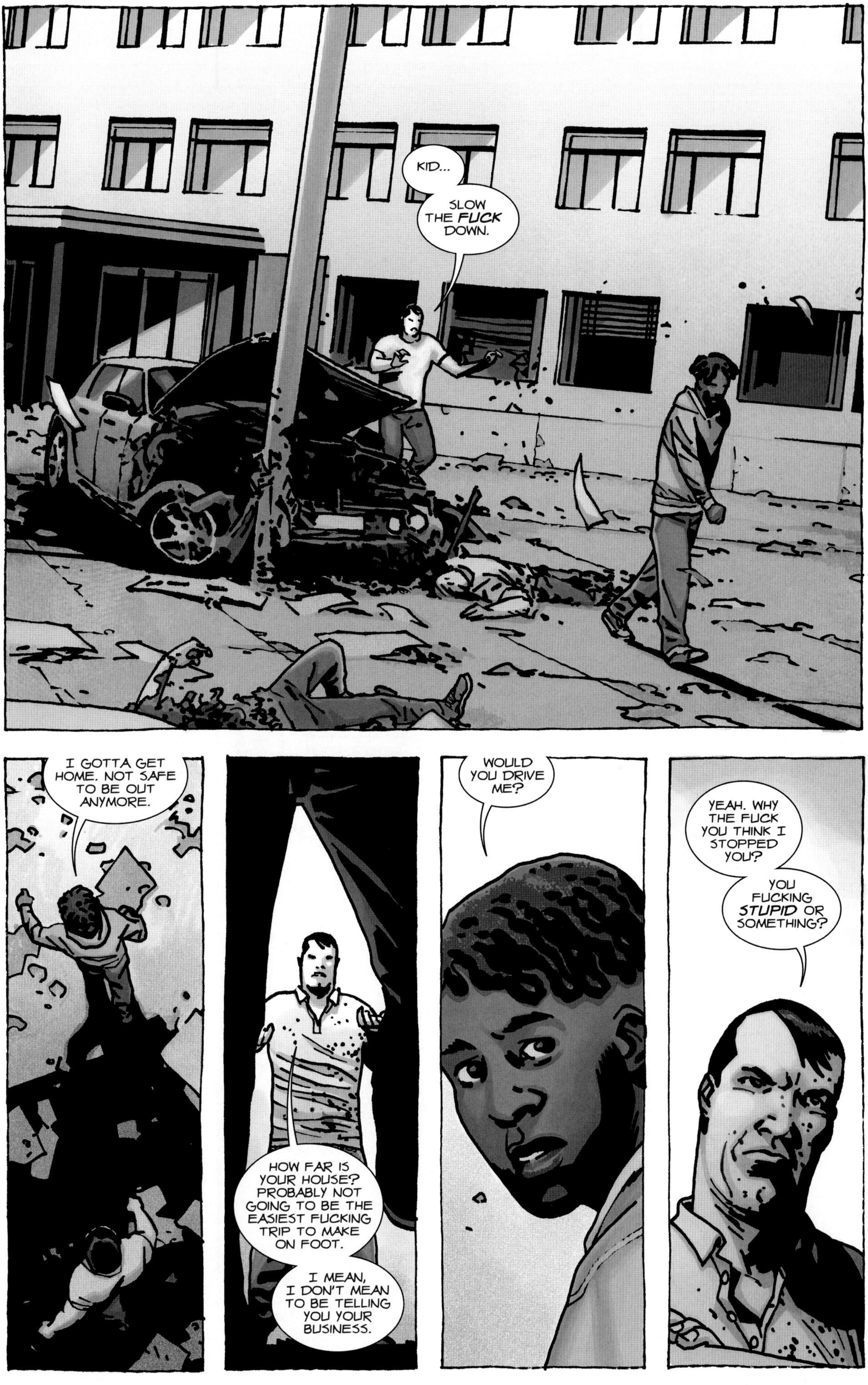
KID...
SLOW THE FUCK DOWN.
I GOTTA GET HOME. NOT SAFE TO BE OUT ANYMORE.
HOW FAR IS YOUR HOUSE? PROBABLY NOT GOING TO BE THE EASIEST FUCKING TRIP TO MAKE ON FOOT.
I MEAN, I DON'T MEAN TO BE TELLING YOU YOUR BUSINESS.
WOULD YOU DRIVE ME?
YEAH. WHY THE FUCK YOU THINK I STOPPED YOU?
YOU FUCKING STUPID OR SOMETHING?

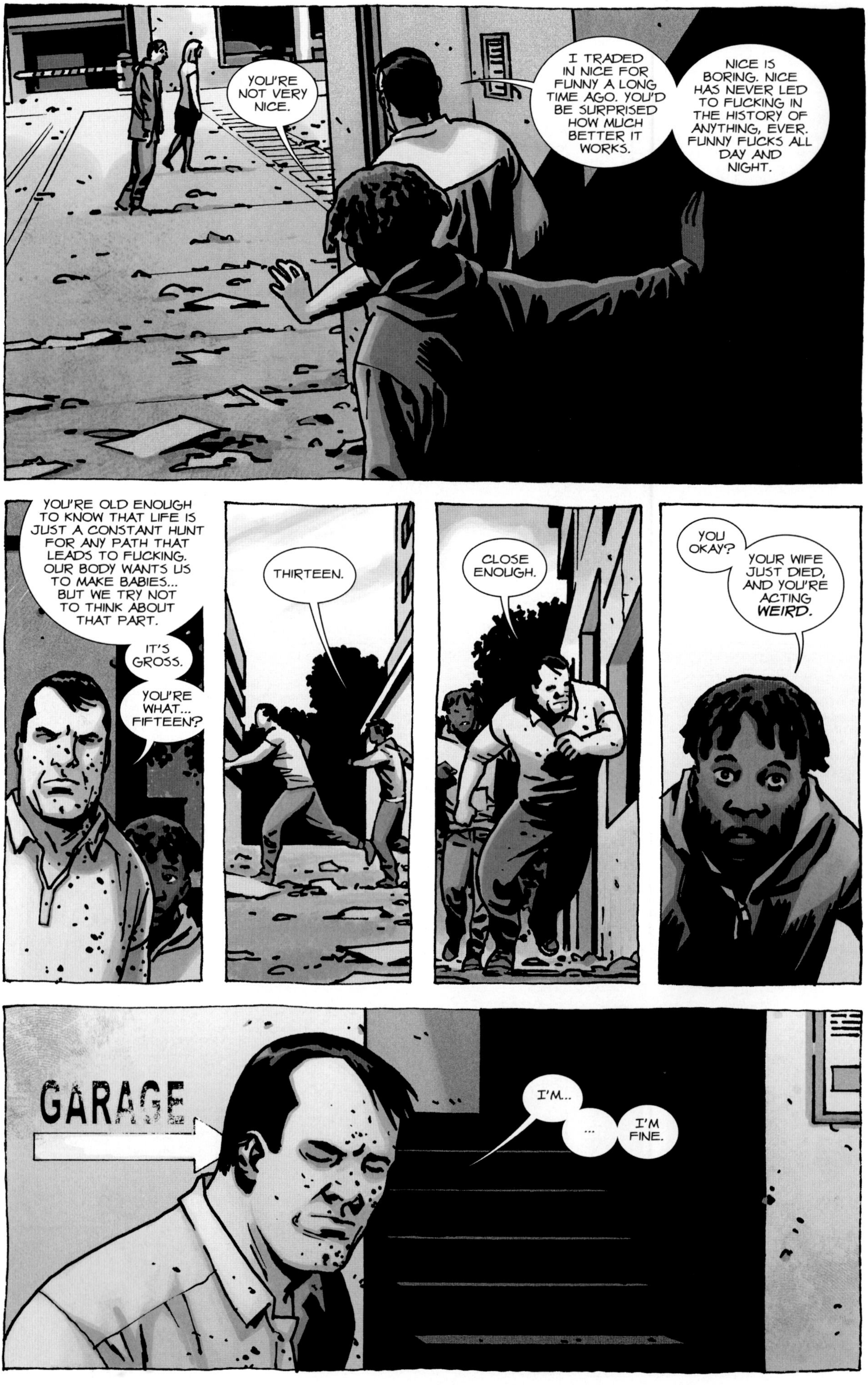
YOU'RE NOT VERY NICE.
I TRADED IN NICE FOR FUNNY A LONG TIME AGO. YOU'D BE SURPRISED HOW MUCH BETTER IT WORKS.
NICE IS BORING. NICE HAS NEVER LED TO FUCKING IN THE HISTORY OF ANYTHING, EVER. FUNNY FUCKS ALL DAY AND NIGHT.
YOU'RE OLD ENOUGH TO KNOW THAT LIFE IS JUST A CONSTANT HUNT FOR ANY PATH THAT LEADS TO FUCKING. OUR BODY WANTS US TO MAKE BABIES... BUT WE TRY NOT TO THINK ABOUT THAT PART.
IT'S GROSS.
YOU'RE WHAT... FIFTEEN?
THIRTEEN.
CLOSE ENOUGH.
YOU OKAY?
YOUR WIFE JUST DIED, AND YOU'RE ACTING *WEIRD.*
GARAGE
I'M...
...
I'M FINE.

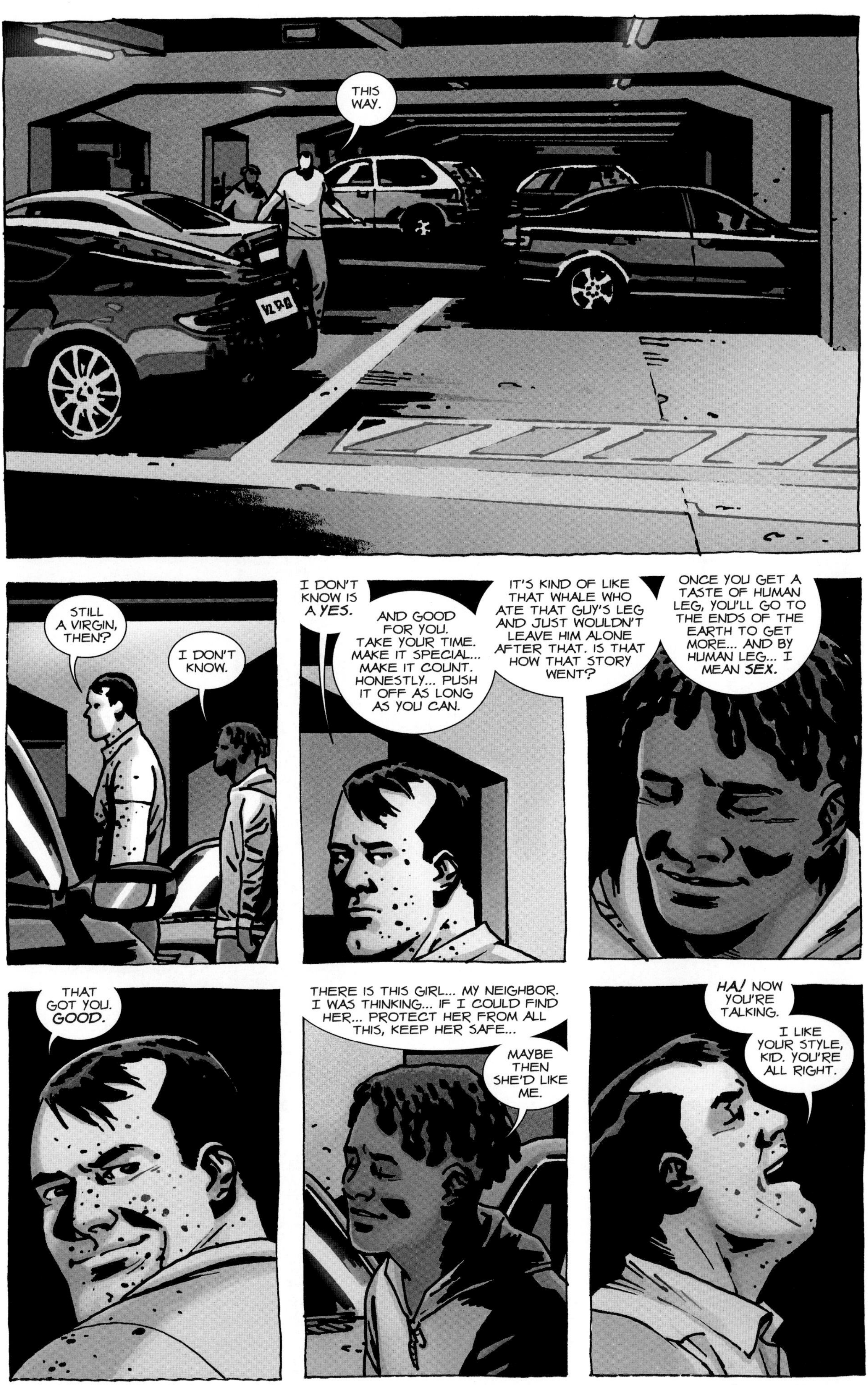
THIS WAY.
STILL A VIRGIN, THEN?
I DON'T KNOW.
I DON'T KNOW IS A YES.
AND GOOD FOR YOU. TAKE YOUR TIME. MAKE IT SPECIAL... MAKE IT COUNT. HONESTLY... PUSH IT OFF AS LONG AS YOU CAN.
IT'S KIND OF LIKE THAT WHALE WHO ATE THAT GUY'S LEG AND JUST WOULDN'T LEAVE HIM ALONE AFTER THAT. IS THAT HOW THAT STORY WENT?
ONCE YOU GET A TASTE OF HUMAN LEG, YOU'LL GO TO THE ENDS OF THE EARTH TO GET MORE... AND BY HUMAN LEG... I MEAN SEX.
THAT GOT YOU. GOOD.
THERE IS THIS GIRL... MY NEIGHBOR. I WAS THINKING... IF I COULD FIND HER... PROTECT HER FROM ALL THIS, KEEP HER SAFE...
MAYBE THEN SHE'D LIKE ME.
HA! NOW YOU'RE TALKING.
I LIKE YOUR STYLE, KID. YOU'RE ALL RIGHT.

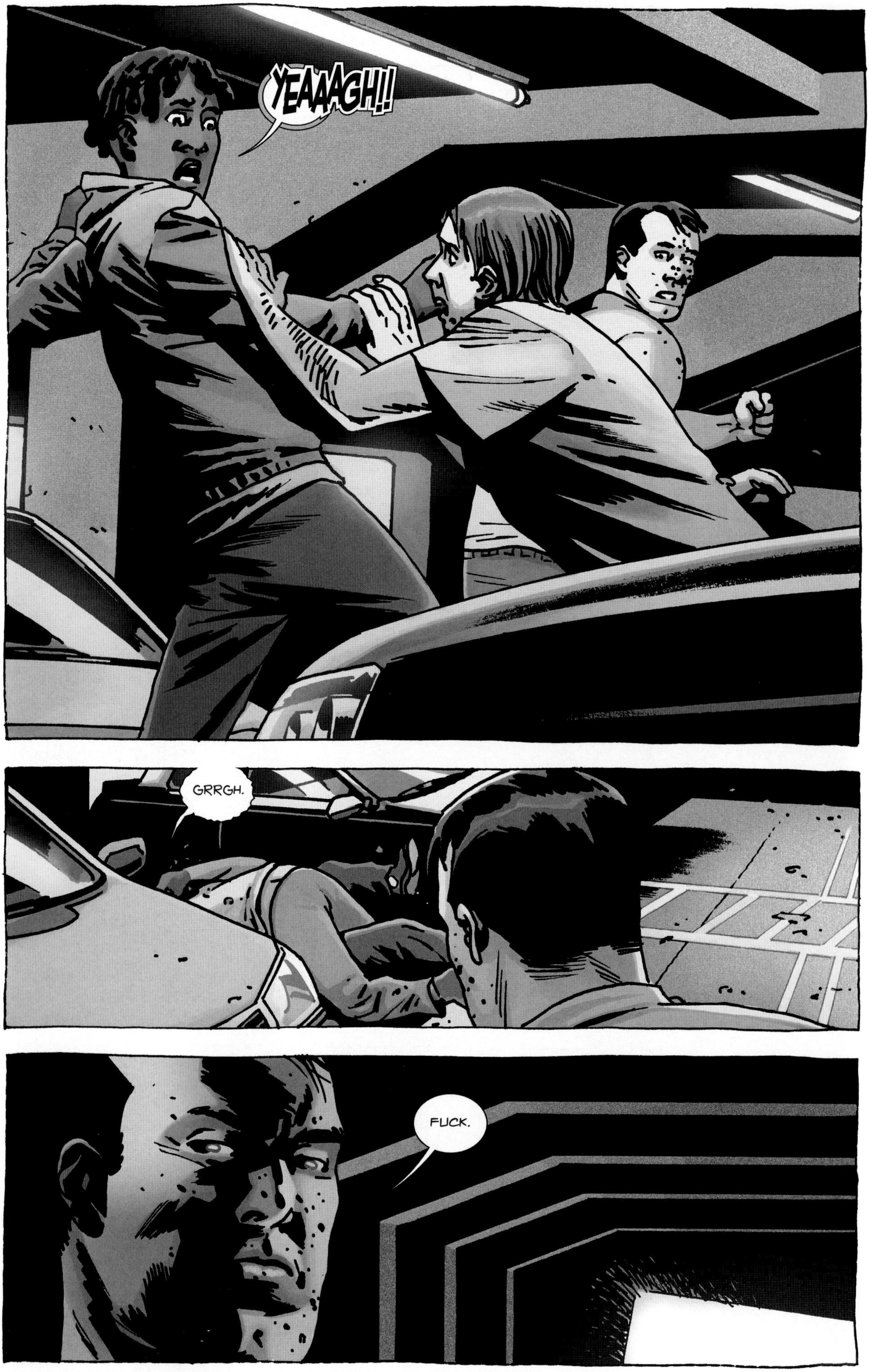
YEAAAGH!!
GRRGH.
FUCK.

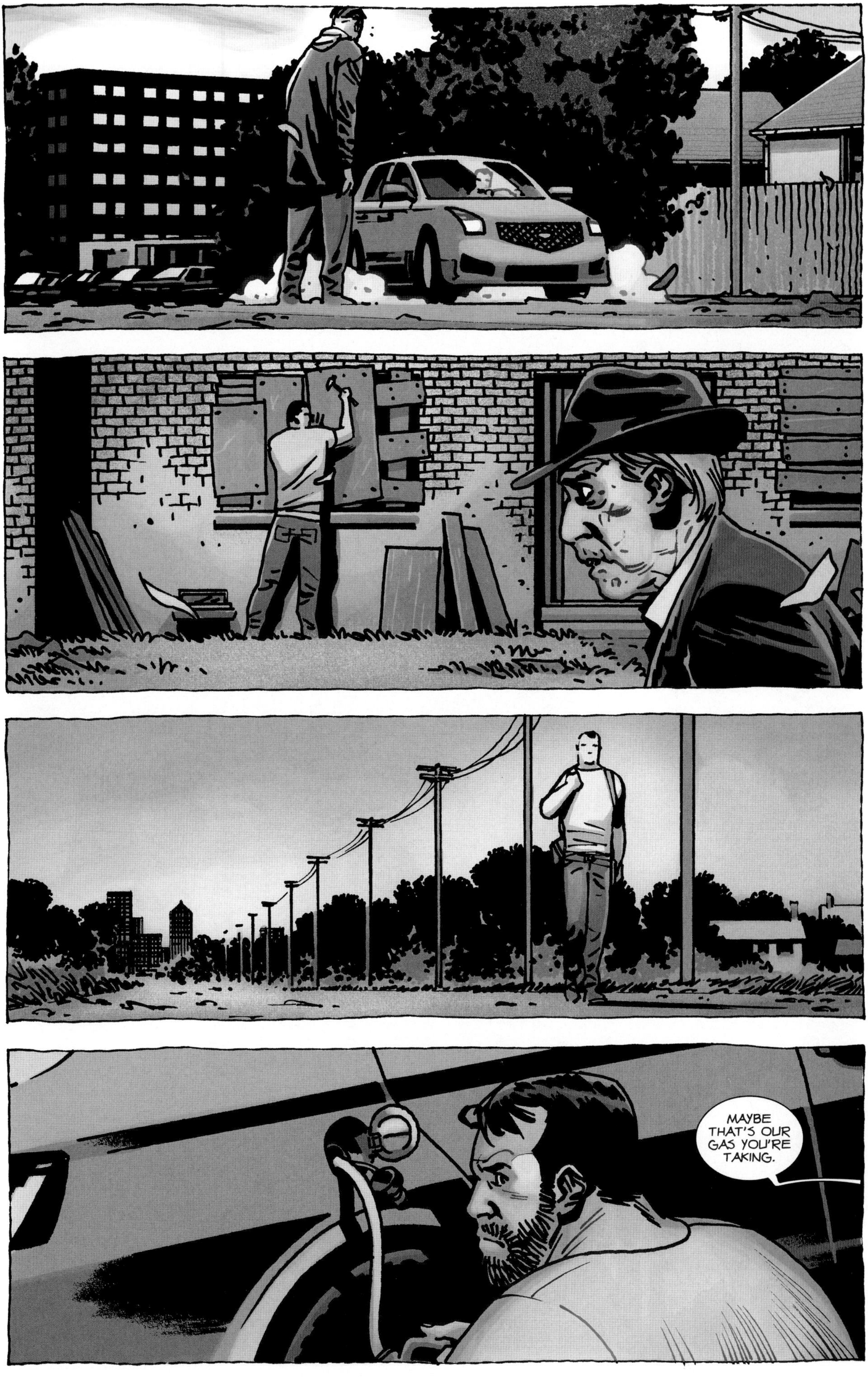
MAYBE THAT'S OUR GAS YOU'RE TAKING.

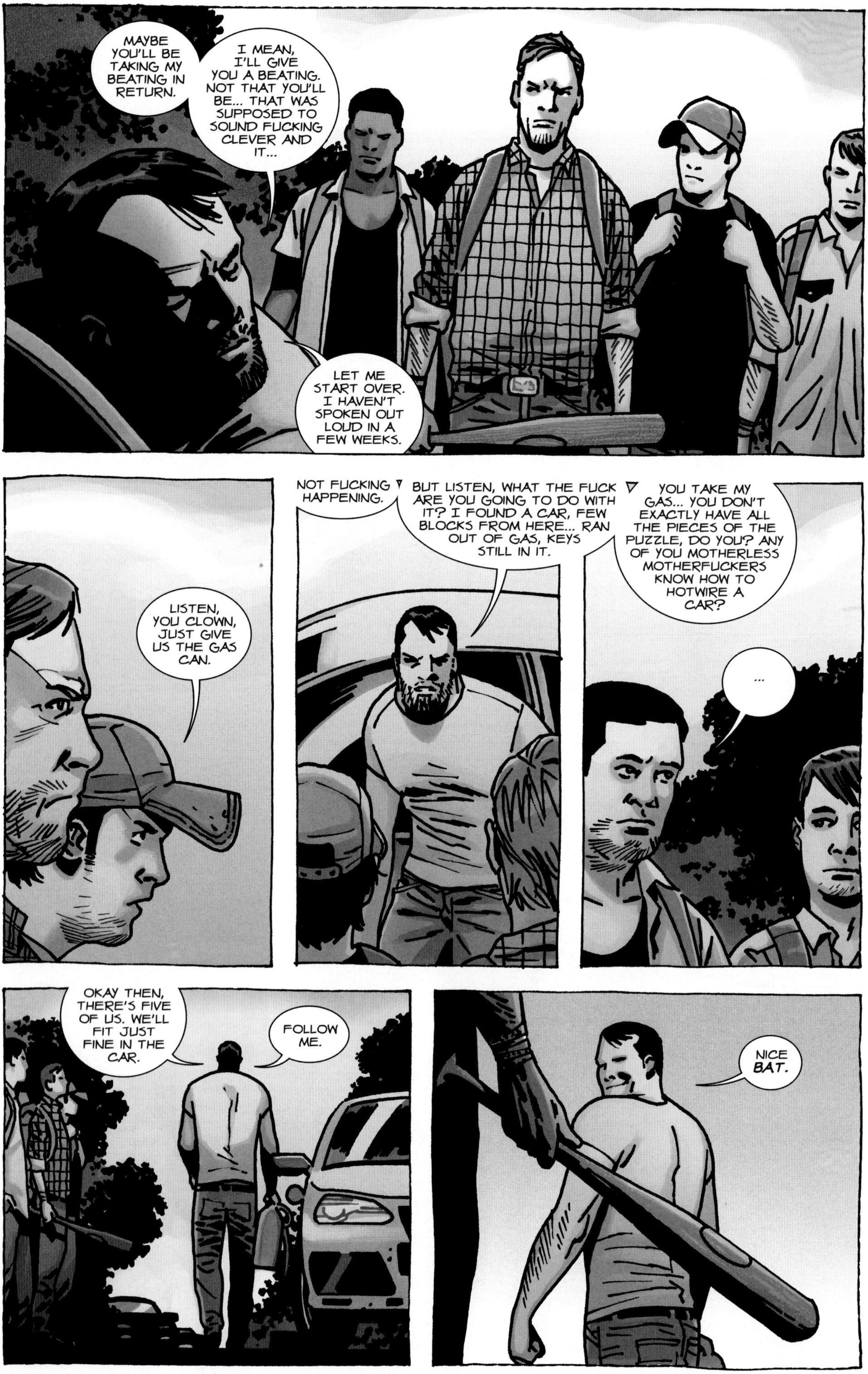
MAYBE YOU'LL BE TAKING MY BEATING IN RETURN.
I MEAN, I'LL GIVE YOU A BEATING. NOT THAT YOU'LL BE... THAT WAS SUPPOSED TO SOUND FUCKING CLEVER AND IT...
LET ME START OVER. I HAVEN'T SPOKEN OUT LOUD IN A FEW WEEKS.
LISTEN, YOU CLOWN, JUST GIVE US THE GAS CAN.
NOT FUCKING HAPPENING.
BUT LISTEN, WHAT THE FUCK ARE YOU GOING TO DO WITH IT? I FOUND A CAR, FEW BLOCKS FROM HERE... RAN OUT OF GAS, KEYS STILL IN IT.
YOU TAKE MY GAS... YOU DON'T EXACTLY HAVE ALL THE PIECES OF THE PUZZLE, DO YOU? ANY OF YOU MOTHERLESS MOTHERFUCKERS KNOW HOW TO HOTWIRE A CAR?
...
OKAY THEN, THERE'S FIVE OF US. WE'LL FIT JUST FINE IN THE CAR.
FOLLOW ME.
NICE BAT.

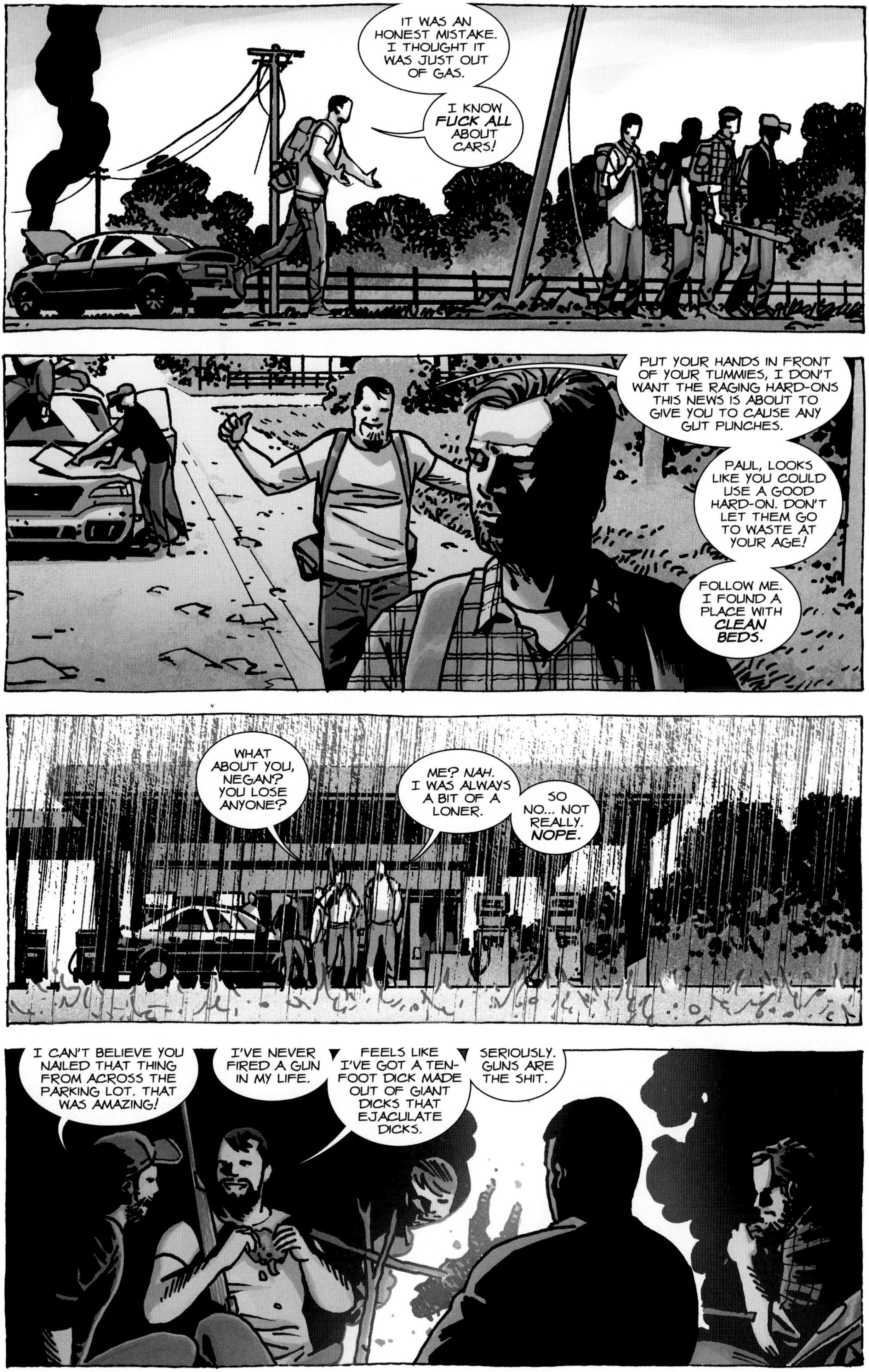
IT WAS AN HONEST MISTAKE. I THOUGHT IT WAS JUST OUT OF GAS.
I KNOW **FUCK ALL** ABOUT CARS!
PUT YOUR HANDS IN FRONT OF YOUR TUMMIES, I DON'T WANT THE RAGING HARD-ONS THIS NEWS IS ABOUT TO GIVE YOU TO CAUSE ANY GUT PUNCHES.
PAUL, LOOKS LIKE YOU COULD USE A GOOD HARD-ON. DON'T LET THEM GO TO WASTE AT YOUR AGE!
FOLLOW ME. I FOUND A PLACE WITH **CLEAN BEDS.**
WHAT ABOUT YOU, NEGAN? YOU LOSE ANYONE?
ME? *NAH.* I WAS ALWAYS A BIT OF A LONER.
SO NO... NOT REALLY. ***NOPE.***
I CAN'T BELIEVE YOU NAILED THAT THING FROM ACROSS THE PARKING LOT. THAT WAS AMAZING!
I'VE NEVER FIRED A GUN IN MY LIFE.
FEELS LIKE I'VE GOT A TEN-FOOT DICK MADE OUT OF GIANT DICKS THAT EJACULATE DICKS.
SERIOUSLY. GUNS ARE THE SHIT.

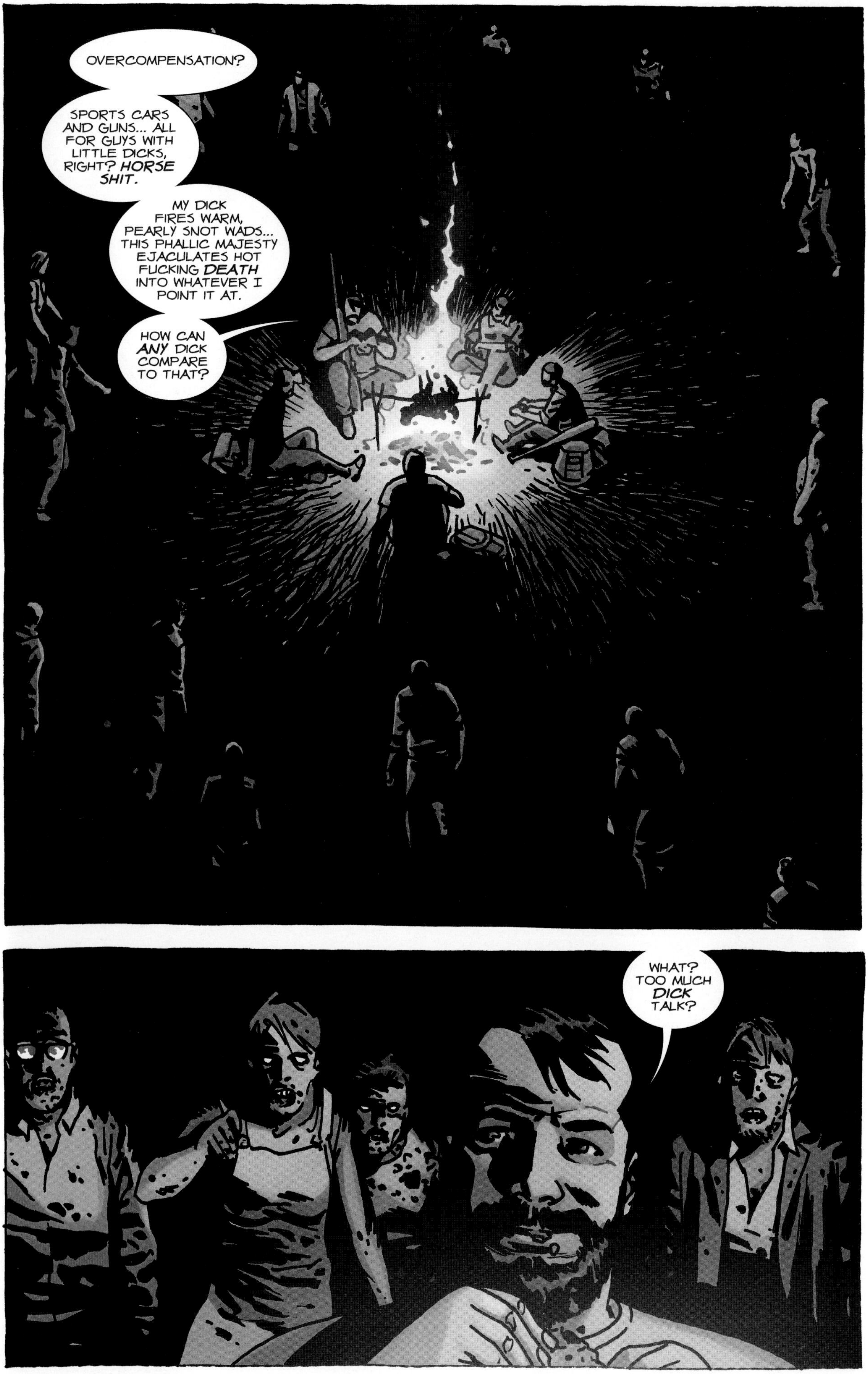
OVERCOMPENSATION?
SPORTS CARS AND GUNS... ALL FOR GUYS WITH LITTLE DICKS, RIGHT? HORSE SHIT.
MY DICK FIRES WARM, PEARLY SNOT WADS... THIS PHALLIC MAJESTY EJACULATES HOT FUCKING DEATH INTO WHATEVER I POINT IT AT.
HOW CAN ANY DICK COMPARE TO THAT?
WHAT? TOO MUCH DICK TALK?

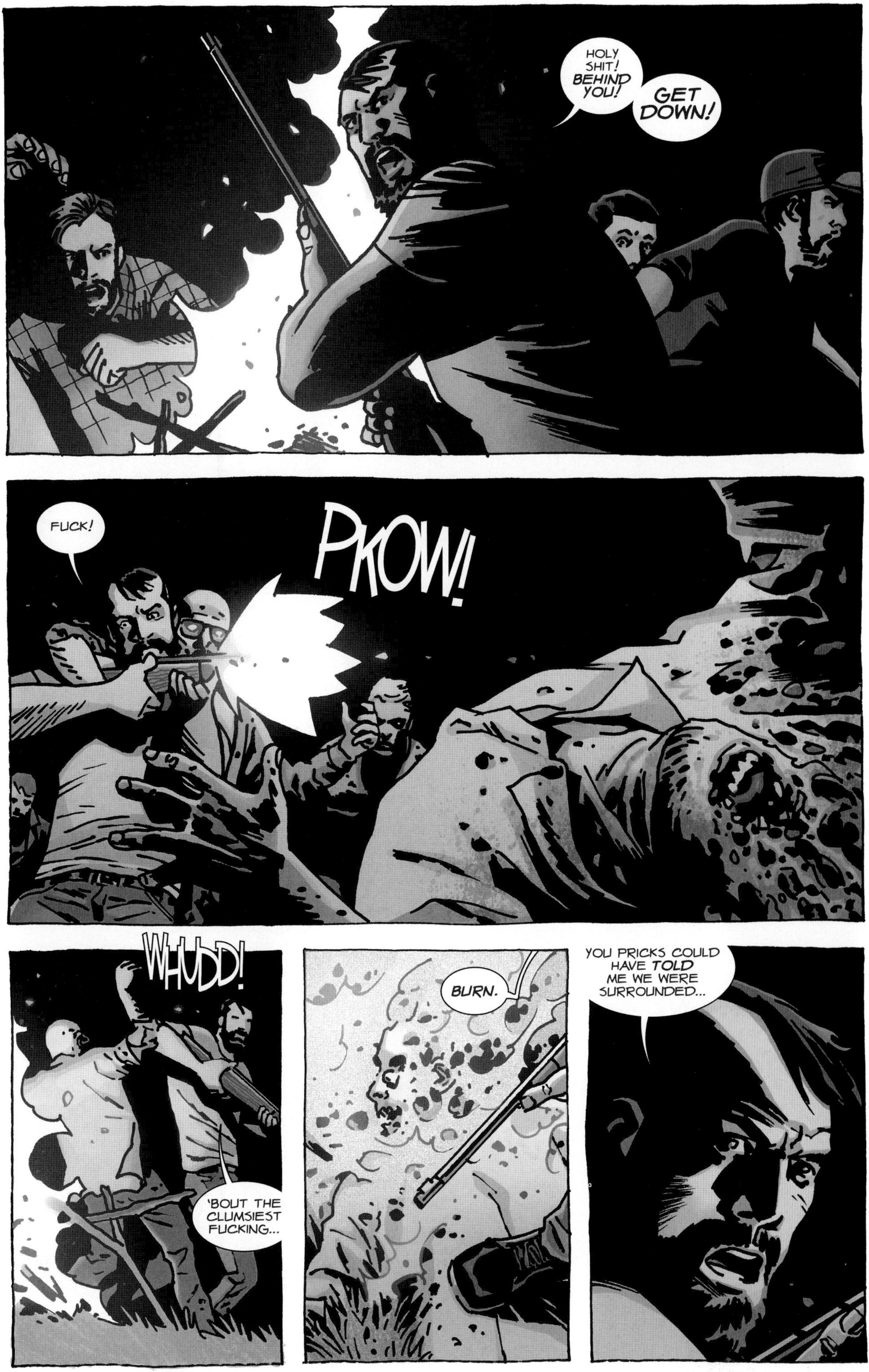
HOLY SHIT! BEHIND YOU!
GET DOWN!
FUCK!
PKOW!
WHUDD!
'BOUT THE CLUMSIEST FUCKING...
BURN.
YOU PRICKS COULD HAVE TOLD ME WE WERE SURROUNDED...

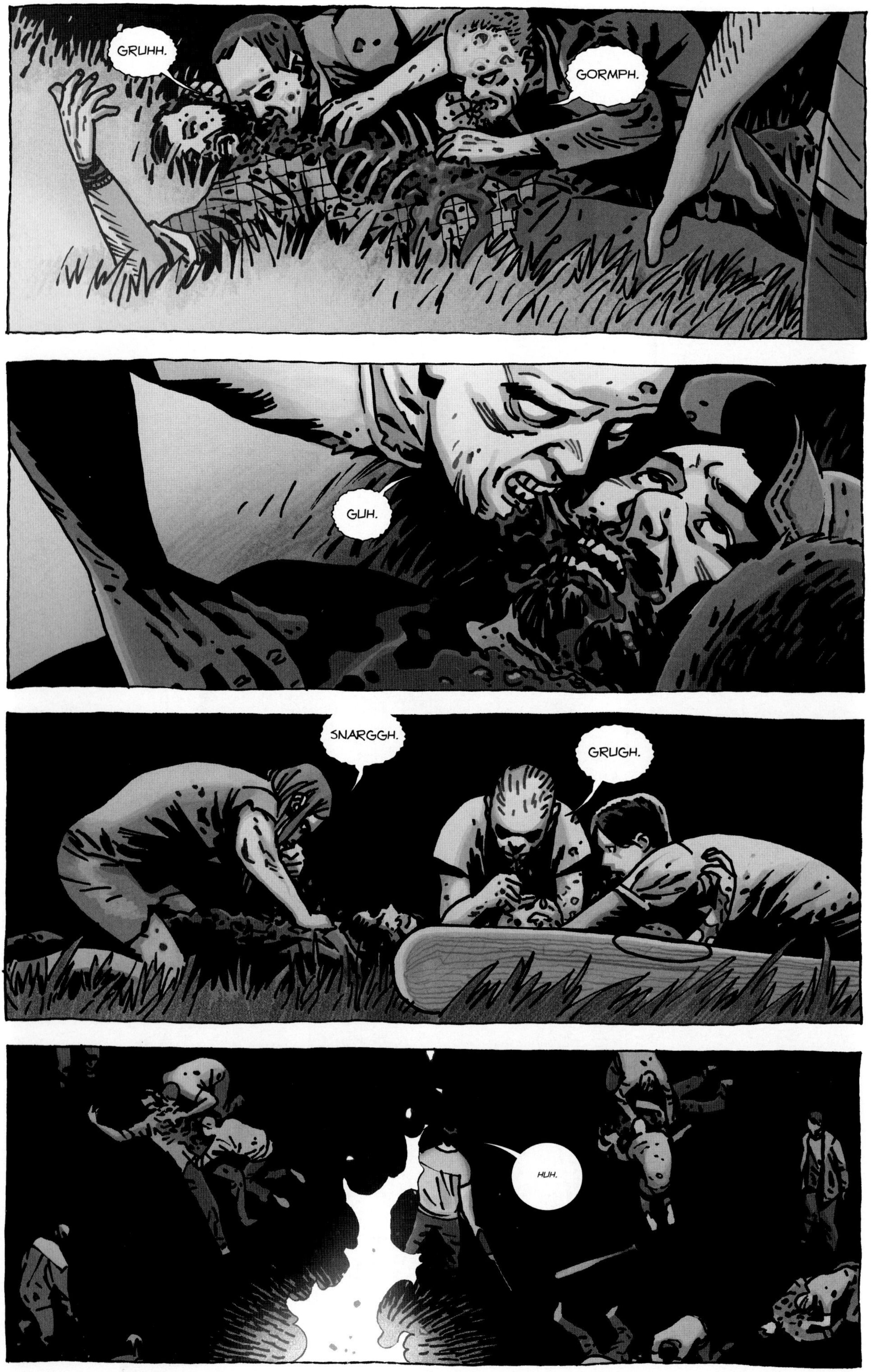
GRUHH.
GORMPH.
GUH.
SNARGGH.
GRUGH.
HUH.

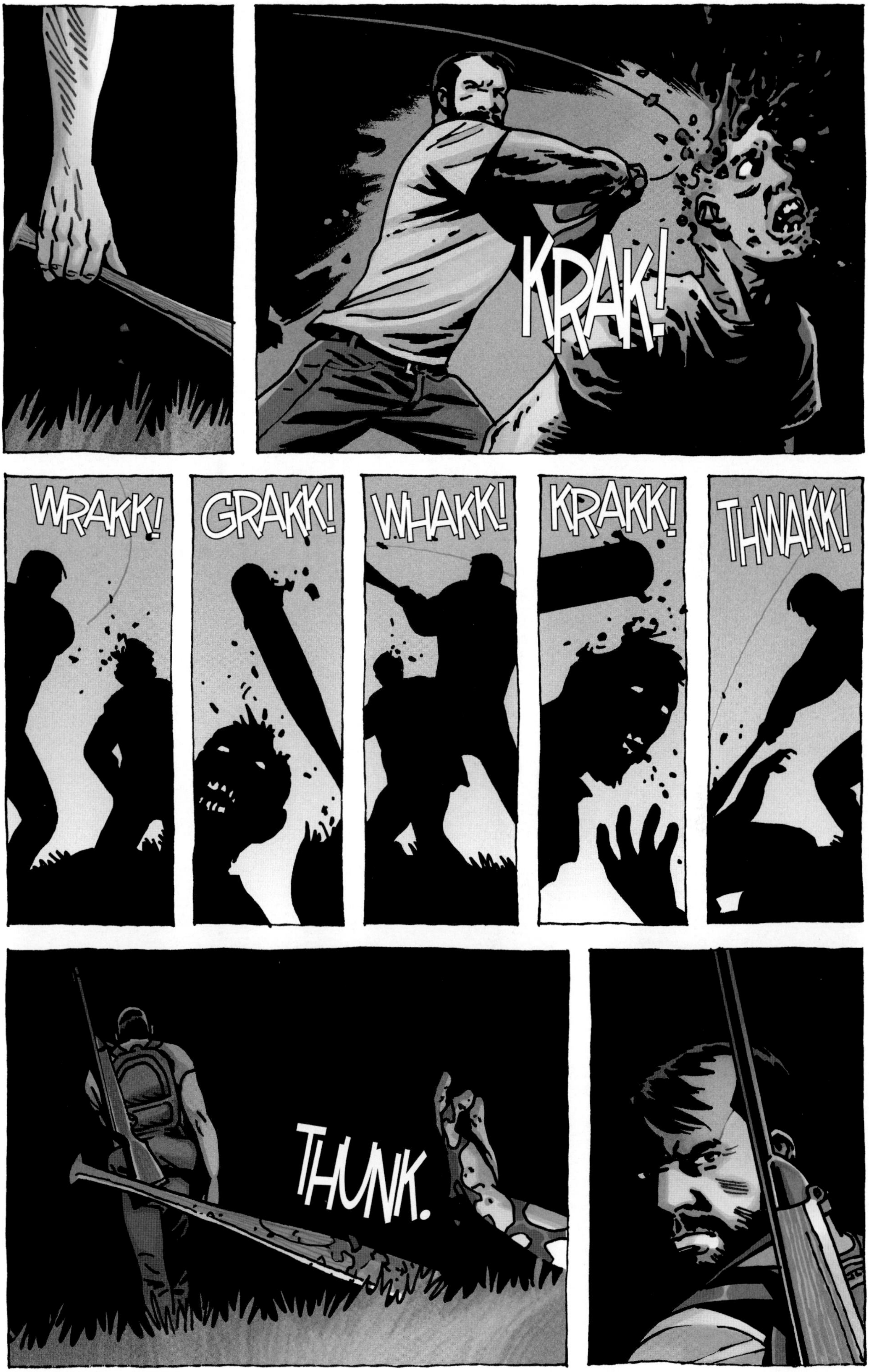
KRAK!
WRAKK!
GRAKK!
WHAKK!
KRAKK!
THWAKK!
THUNK.

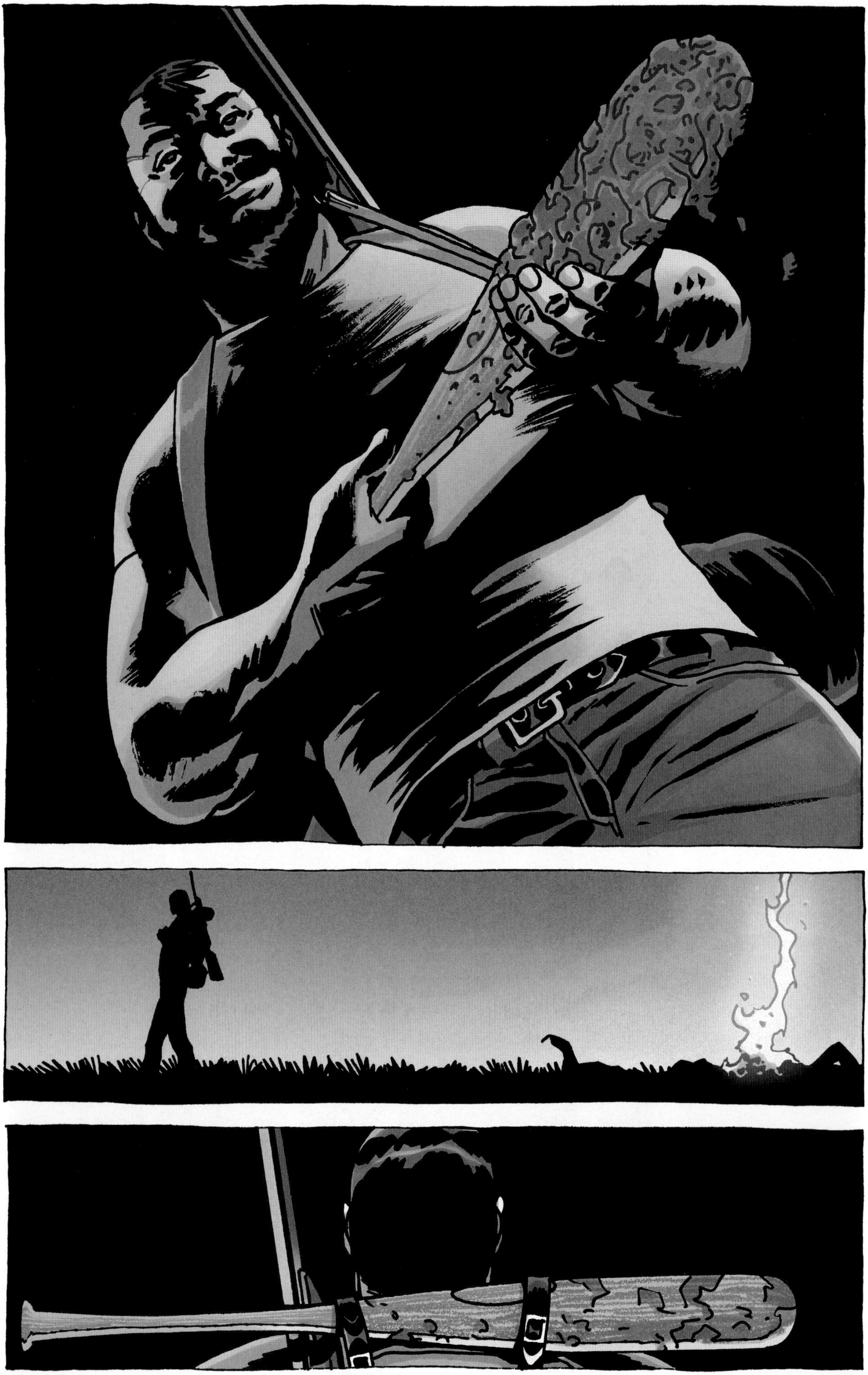

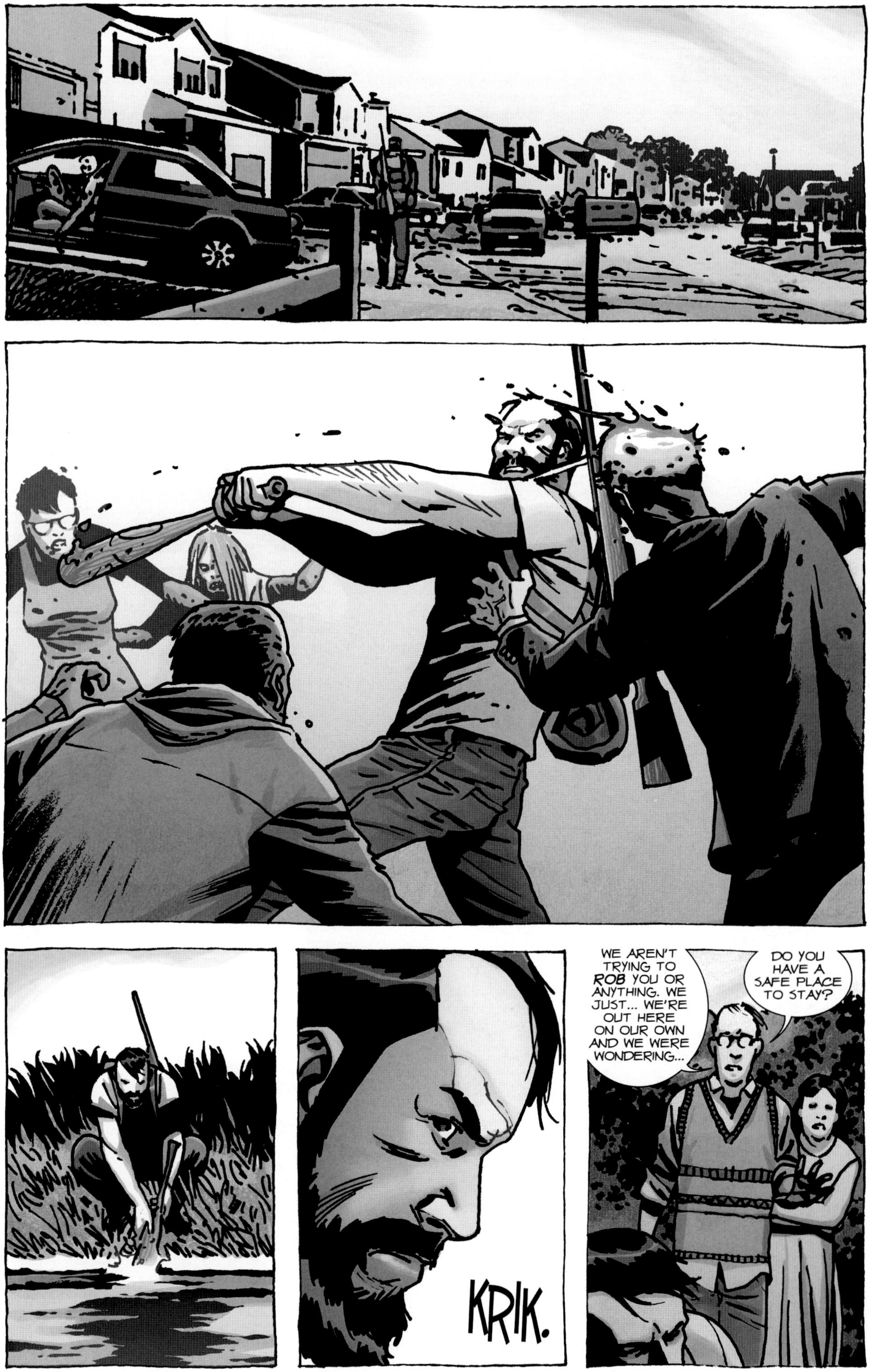

WE AREN'T TRYING TO ROB YOU OR ANYTHING. WE JUST... WE'RE OUT HERE ON OUR OWN AND WE WERE WONDERING...
DO YOU HAVE A SAFE PLACE TO STAY?
KRIK.

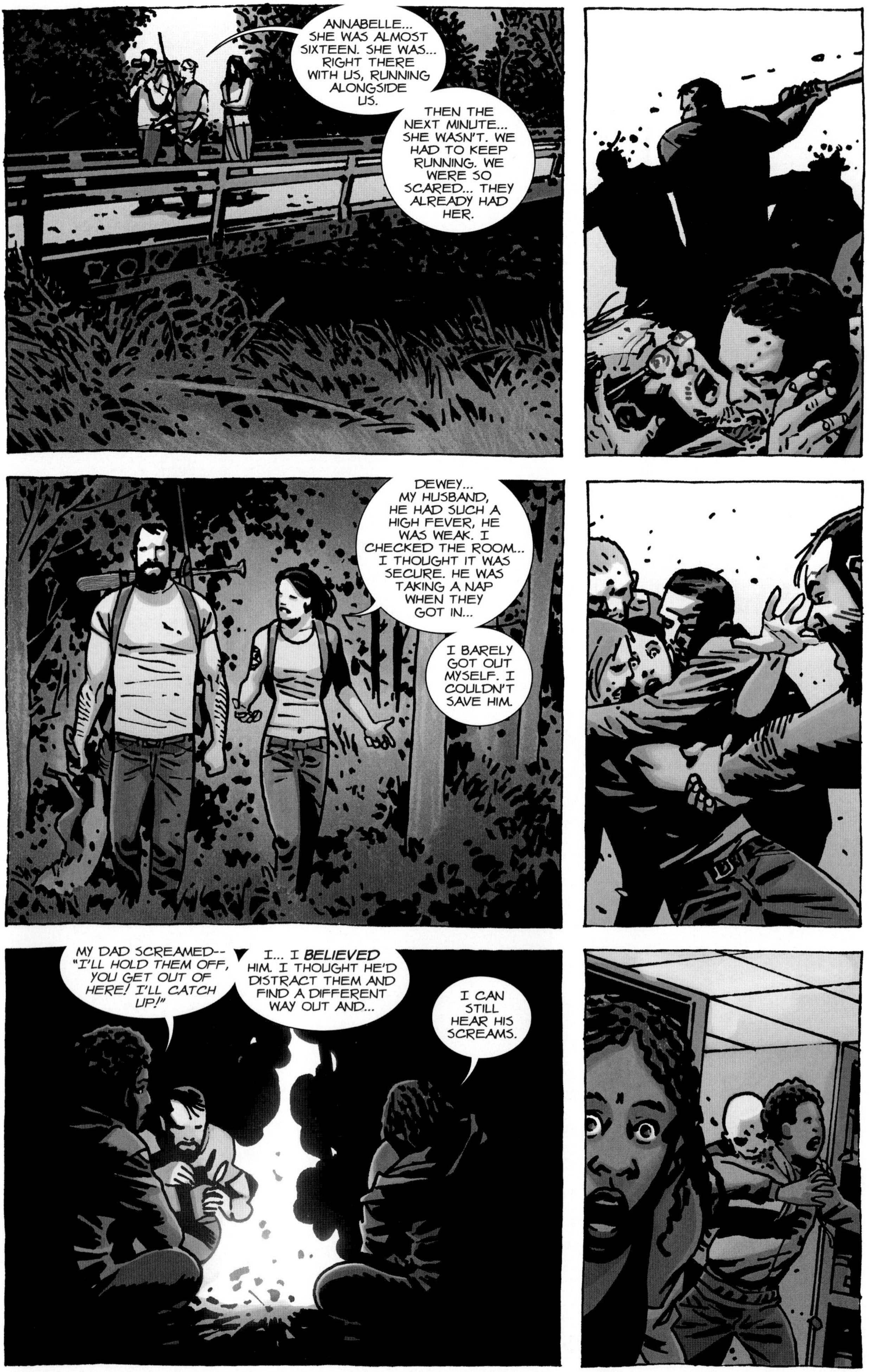
ANNABELLE... SHE WAS ALMOST SIXTEEN. SHE WAS... RIGHT THERE WITH US, RUNNING ALONGSIDE US.
THEN THE NEXT MINUTE... SHE WASN'T. WE HAD TO KEEP RUNNING. WE WERE SO SCARED... THEY ALREADY HAD HER.
DEWEY... MY HUSBAND, HE HAD SUCH A HIGH FEVER, HE WAS WEAK. I CHECKED THE ROOM... I THOUGHT IT WAS SECURE. HE WAS TAKING A NAP WHEN THEY GOT IN...
I BARELY GOT OUT MYSELF. I COULDN'T SAVE HIM.
MY DAD SCREAMED-- "I'LL HOLD THEM OFF, YOU GET OUT OF HERE! I'LL CATCH UP!"
I... I *BELIEVED* HIM. I THOUGHT HE'D DISTRACT THEM AND FIND A DIFFERENT WAY OUT AND...
I CAN STILL HEAR HIS SCREAMS.

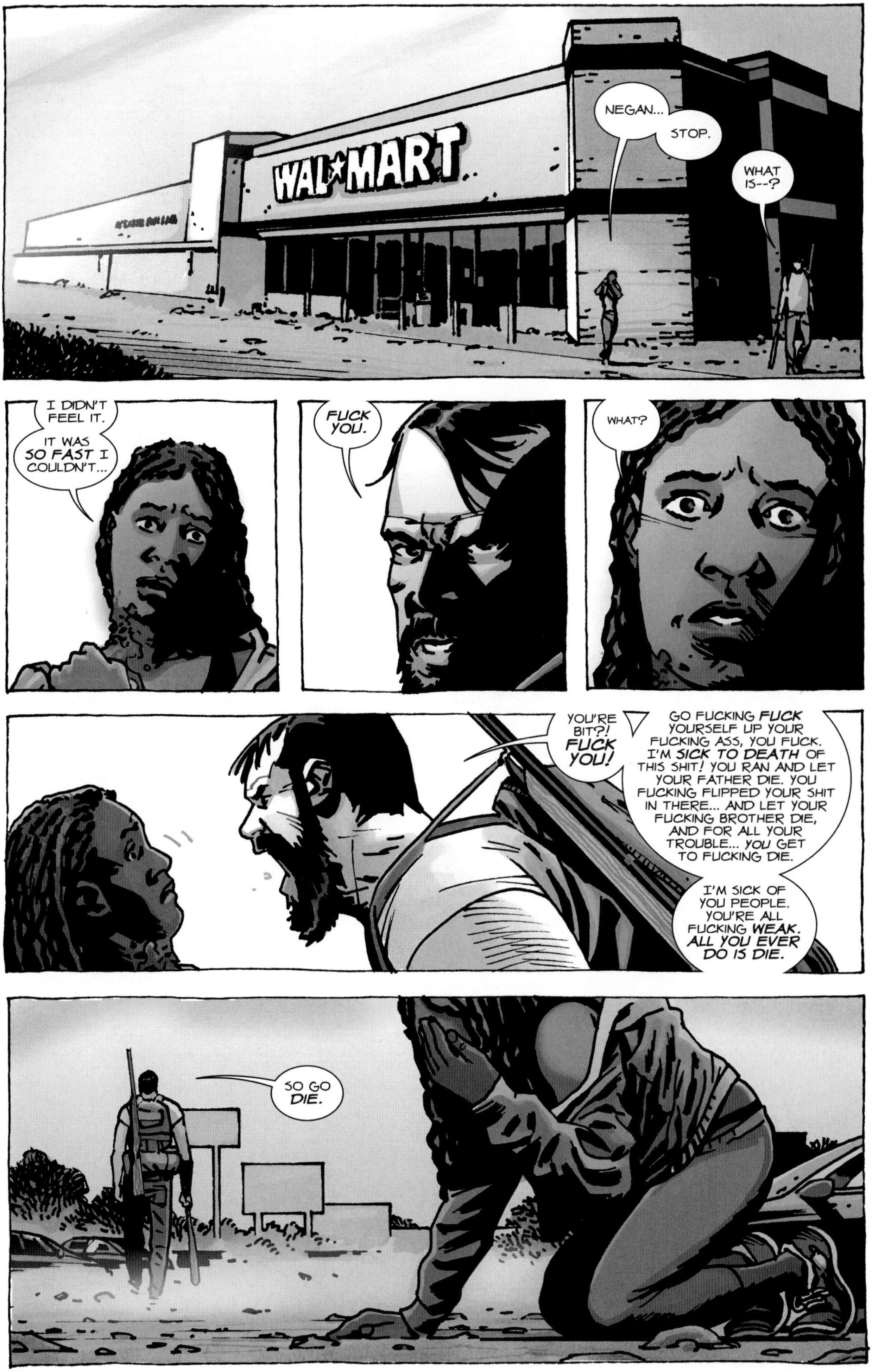
WAL★MART
NEGAN...
STOP.
WHAT IS--?
I DIDN'T FEEL IT.
IT WAS SO FAST I COULDN'T...
FUCK YOU.
WHAT?
YOU'RE BIT?! FUCK YOU!
GO FUCKING FUCK YOURSELF UP YOUR FUCKING ASS, YOU FUCK. I'M SICK TO DEATH OF THIS SHIT! YOU RAN AND LET YOUR FATHER DIE. YOU FUCKING FLIPPED YOUR SHIT IN THERE... AND LET YOUR FUCKING BROTHER DIE, AND FOR ALL YOUR TROUBLE... YOU GET TO FUCKING DIE.
I'M SICK OF YOU PEOPLE. YOU'RE ALL FUCKING WEAK. ALL YOU EVER DO IS DIE.
SO GO DIE.

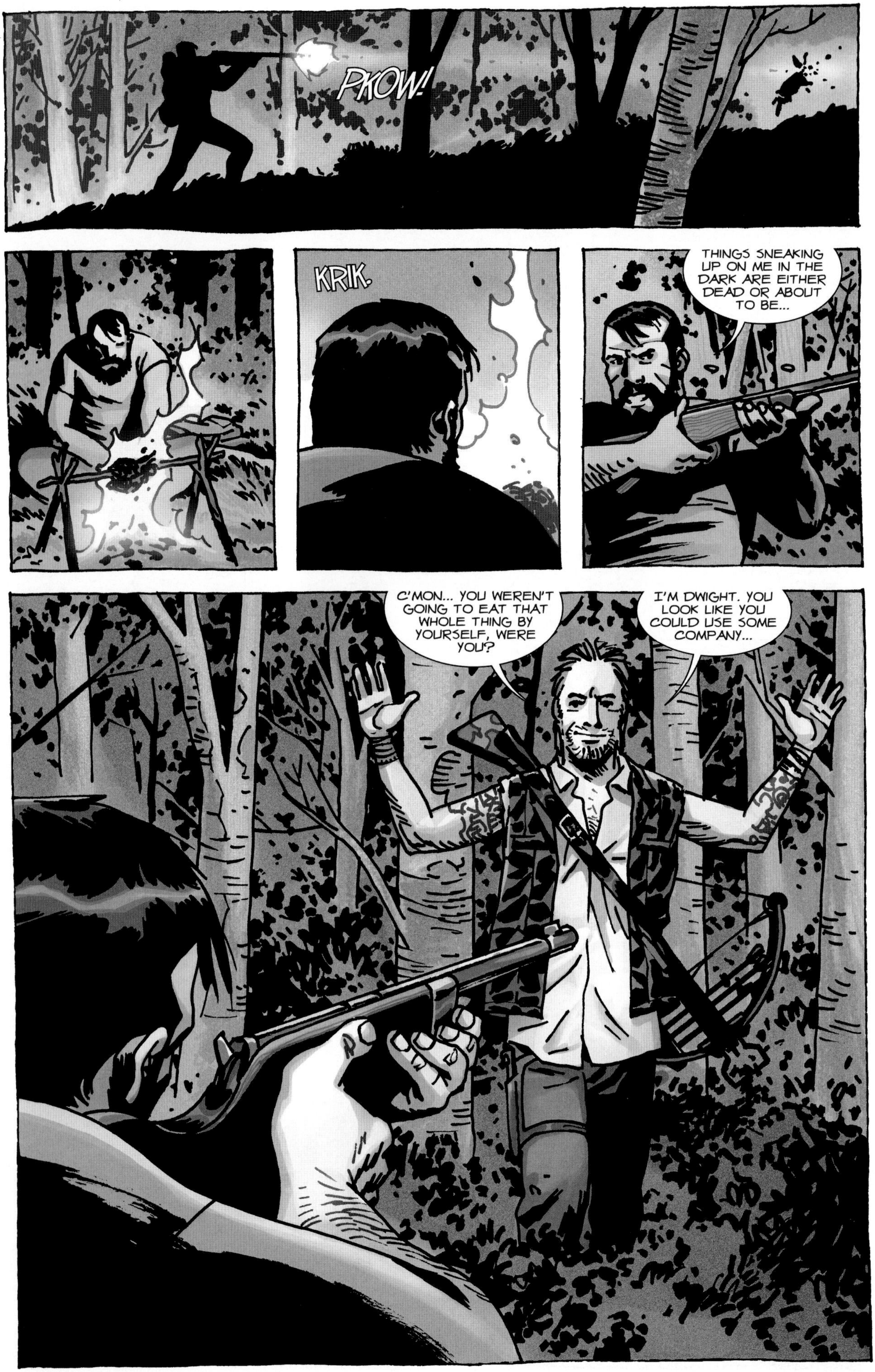
PKOW!
KRIK.
THINGS SNEAKING UP ON ME IN THE DARK ARE EITHER DEAD OR ABOUT TO BE...
C'MON... YOU WEREN'T GOING TO EAT THAT WHOLE THING BY YOURSELF, WERE YOU?
I'M DWIGHT. YOU LOOK LIKE YOU COULD USE SOME COMPANY...

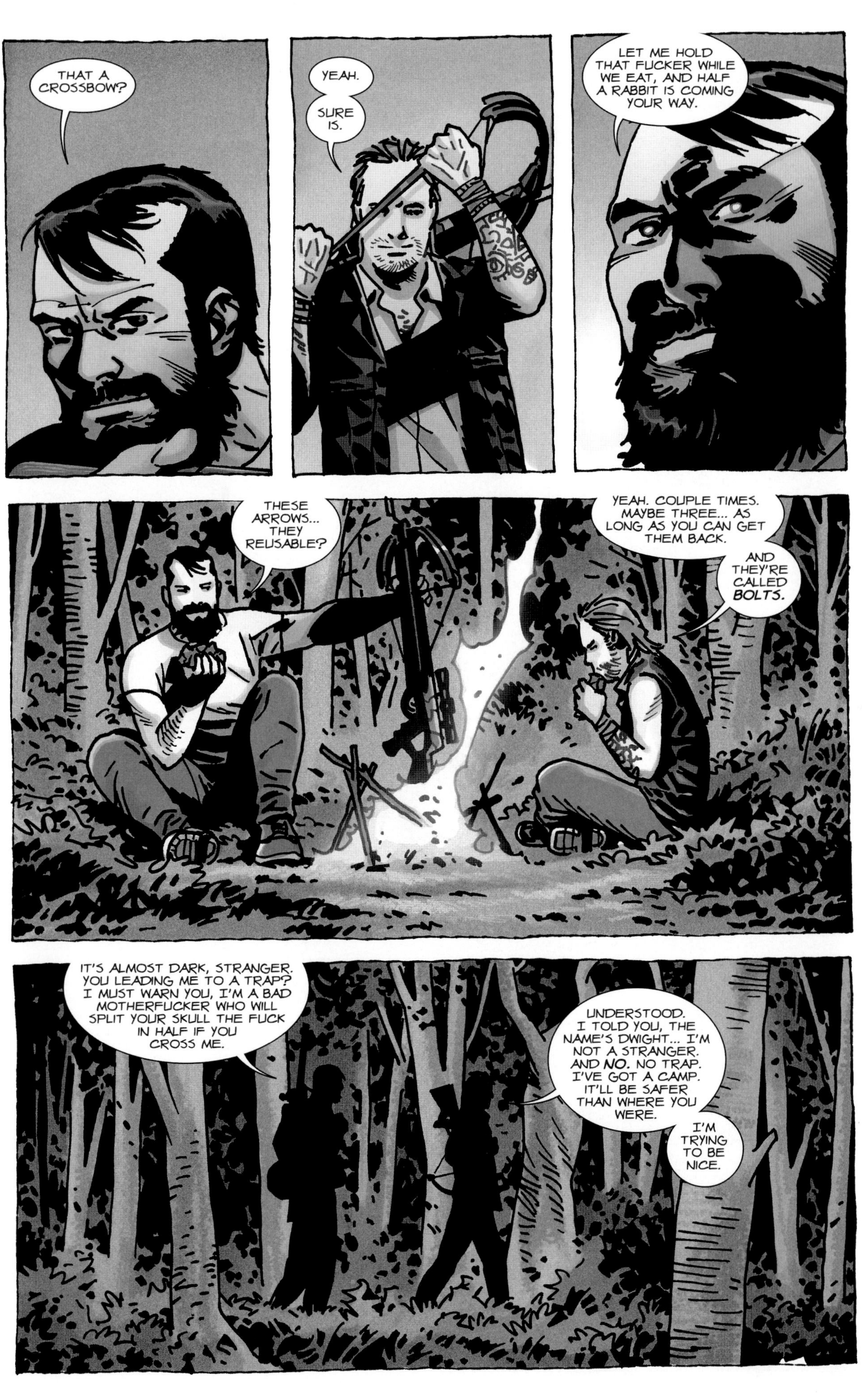
THAT A CROSSBOW?
YEAH.
SURE IS.
LET ME HOLD THAT FUCKER WHILE WE EAT, AND HALF A RABBIT IS COMING YOUR WAY.
THESE ARROWS... THEY REUSABLE?
YEAH. COUPLE TIMES. MAYBE THREE... AS LONG AS YOU CAN GET THEM BACK.
AND THEY'RE CALLED *BOLTS.*
IT'S ALMOST DARK, STRANGER. YOU LEADING ME TO A TRAP? I MUST WARN YOU, I'M A BAD MOTHERFUCKER WHO WILL SPLIT YOUR SKULL THE FUCK IN HALF IF YOU CROSS ME.
UNDERSTOOD. I TOLD YOU, THE NAME'S DWIGHT... I'M NOT A STRANGER. AND *NO.* NO TRAP. I'VE GOT A CAMP. IT'LL BE SAFER THAN WHERE YOU WERE.
I'M TRYING TO BE NICE.

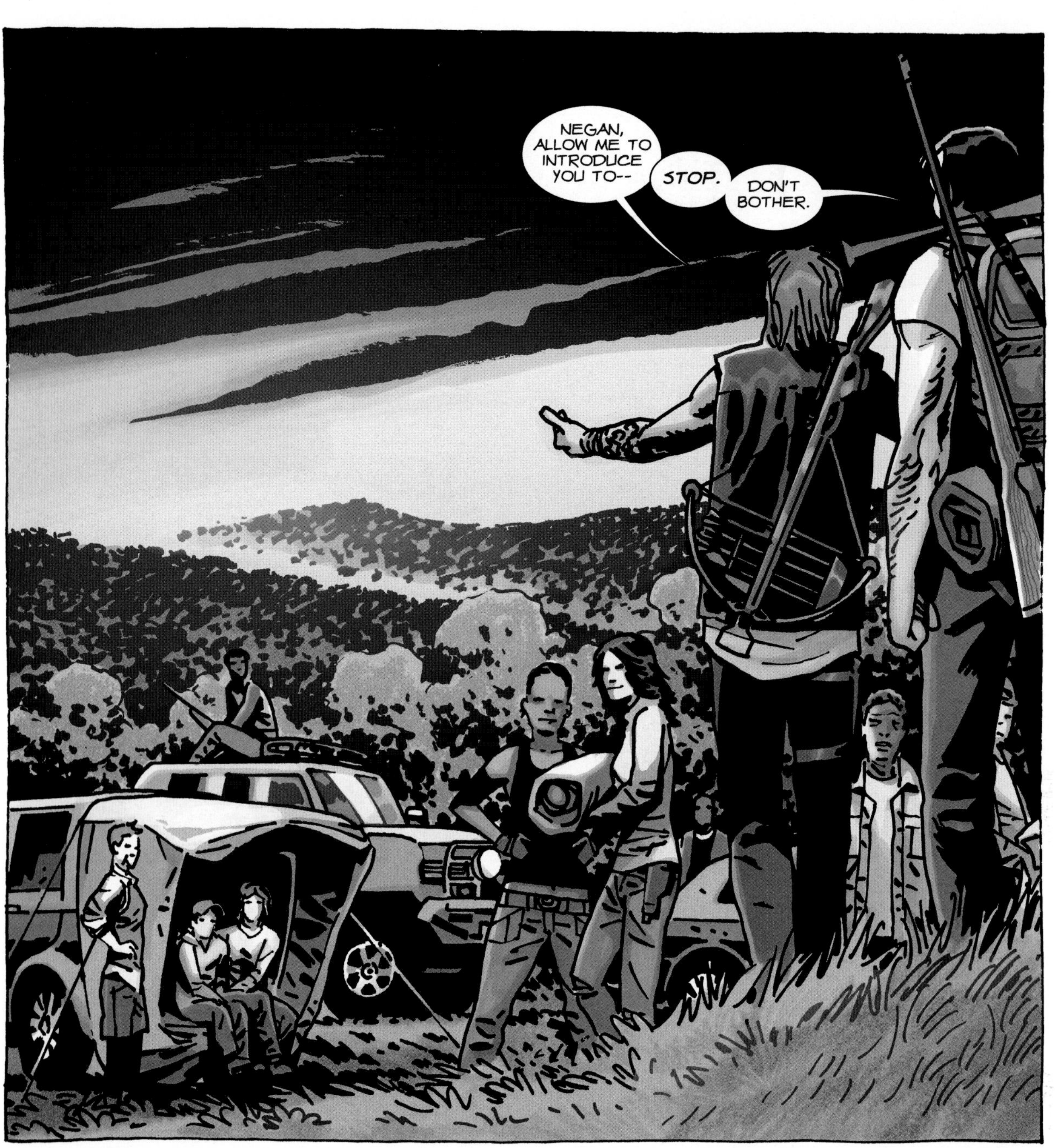
NEGAN, ALLOW ME TO INTRODUCE YOU TO--
STOP.
DON'T BOTHER.

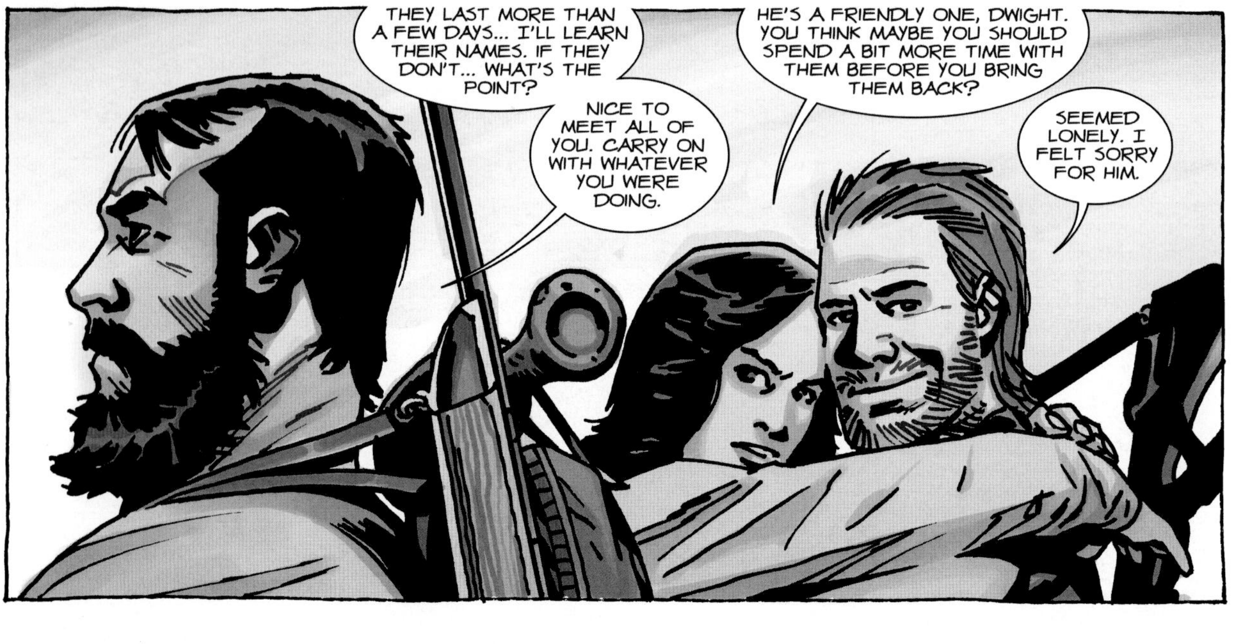
THEY LAST MORE THAN A FEW DAYS... I'LL LEARN THEIR NAMES. IF THEY DON'T... WHAT'S THE POINT?
NICE TO MEET ALL OF YOU. CARRY ON WITH WHATEVER YOU WERE DOING.
HE'S A FRIENDLY ONE, DWIGHT. YOU THINK MAYBE YOU SHOULD SPEND A BIT MORE TIME WITH THEM BEFORE YOU BRING THEM BACK?
SEEMED LONELY. I FELT SORRY FOR HIM.

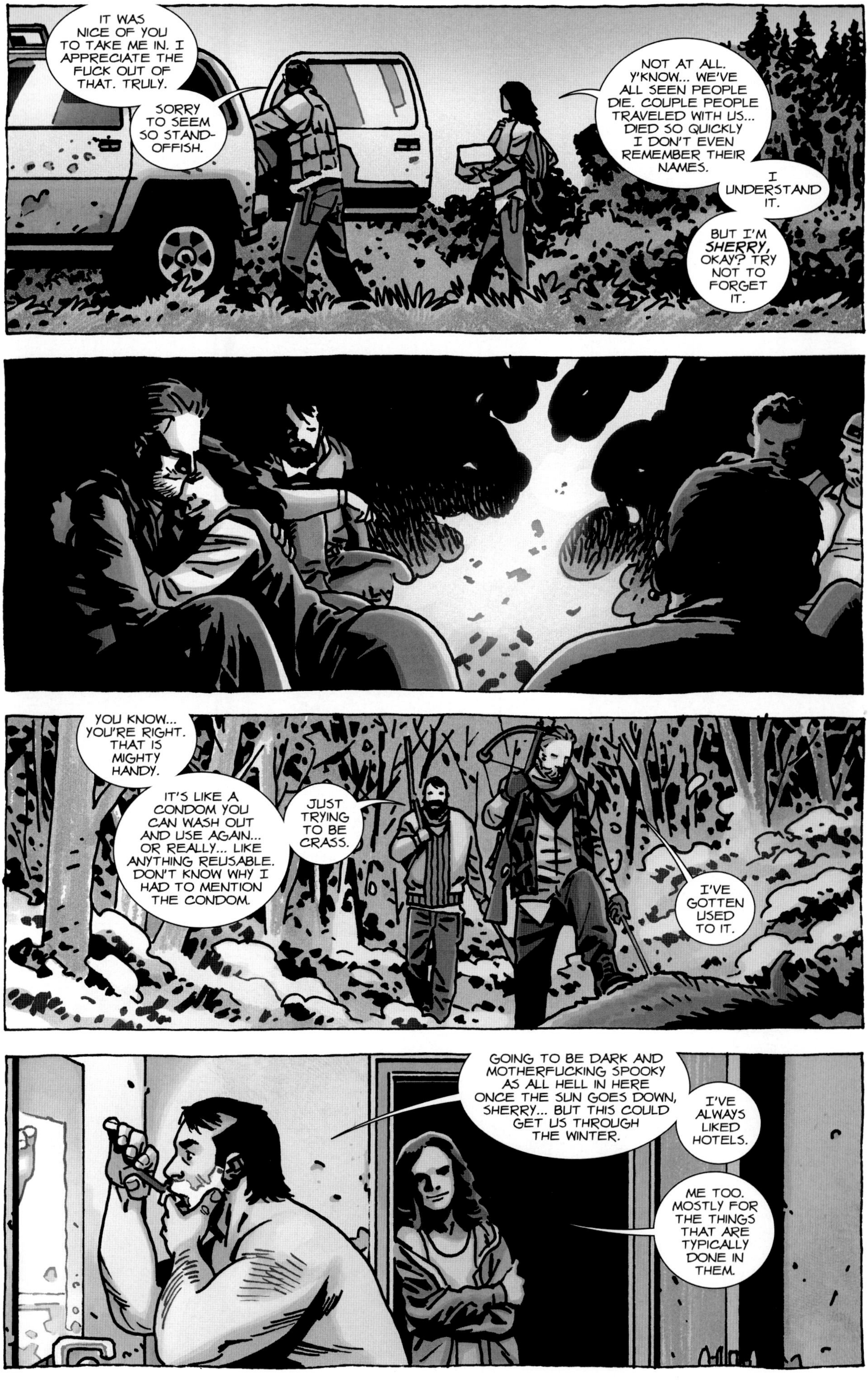
IT WAS NICE OF YOU TO TAKE ME IN. I APPRECIATE THE FUCK OUT OF THAT. TRULY.
SORRY TO SEEM SO STAND-OFFISH.
NOT AT ALL. Y'KNOW... WE'VE ALL SEEN PEOPLE DIE. COUPLE PEOPLE TRAVELED WITH US... DIED SO QUICKLY I DON'T EVEN REMEMBER THEIR NAMES.
I UNDERSTAND IT.
BUT I'M SHERRY, OKAY? TRY NOT TO FORGET IT.
YOU KNOW... YOU'RE RIGHT. THAT IS MIGHTY HANDY.
IT'S LIKE A CONDOM YOU CAN WASH OUT AND USE AGAIN... OR REALLY... LIKE ANYTHING REUSABLE. DON'T KNOW WHY I HAD TO MENTION THE CONDOM.
JUST TRYING TO BE CRASS.
I'VE GOTTEN USED TO IT.
GOING TO BE DARK AND MOTHERFUCKING SPOOKY AS ALL HELL IN HERE ONCE THE SUN GOES DOWN, SHERRY... BUT THIS COULD GET US THROUGH THE WINTER.
I'VE ALWAYS LIKED HOTELS.
ME TOO. MOSTLY FOR THE THINGS THAT ARE TYPICALLY DONE IN THEM.

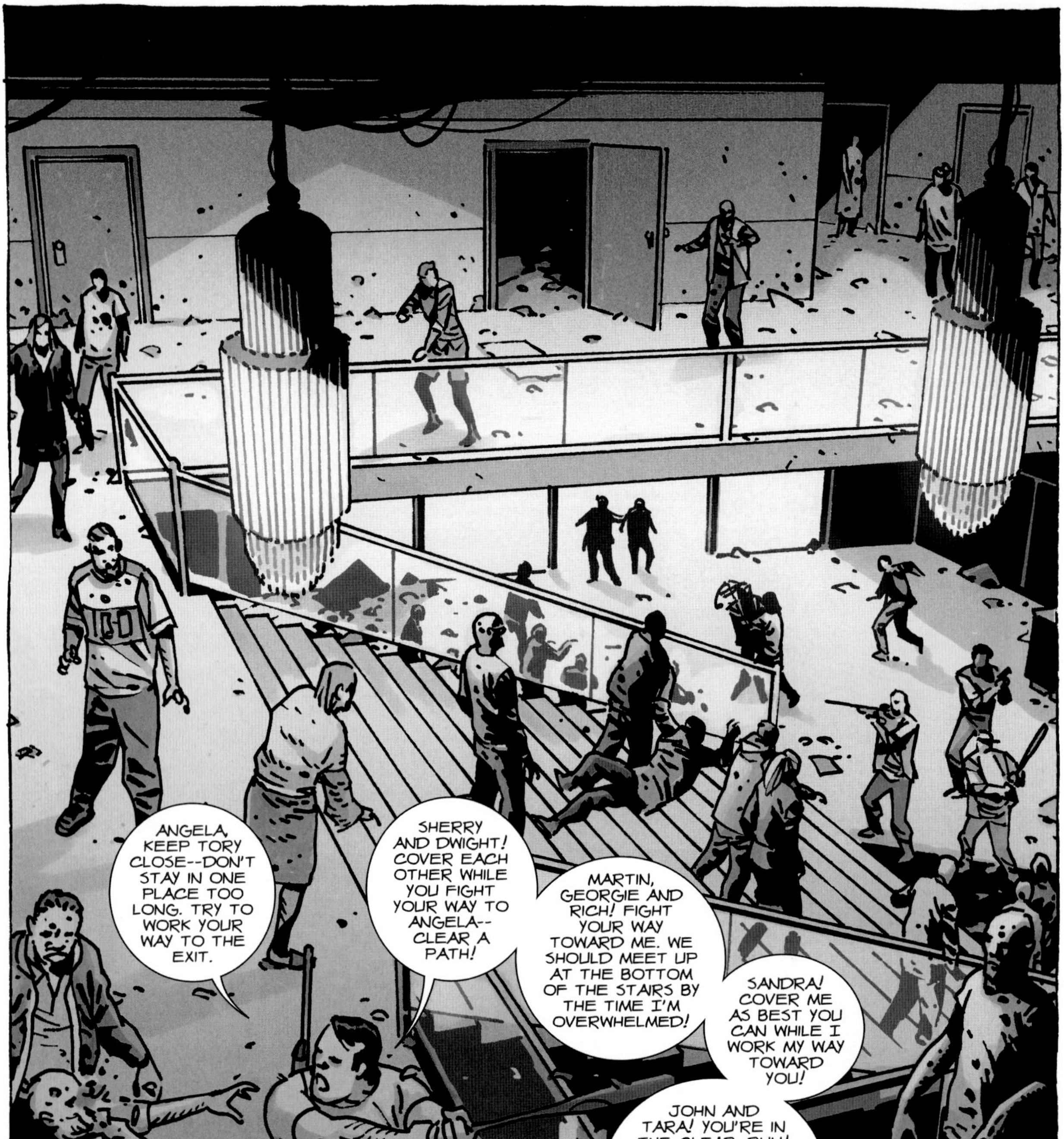
ANGELA, KEEP TORY CLOSE--DON'T STAY IN ONE PLACE TOO LONG. TRY TO WORK YOUR WAY TO THE EXIT.
SHERRY AND DWIGHT! COVER EACH OTHER WHILE YOU FIGHT YOUR WAY TO ANGELA-- CLEAR A PATH!
MARTIN, GEORGIE AND RICH! FIGHT YOUR WAY TOWARD ME. WE SHOULD MEET UP AT THE BOTTOM OF THE STAIRS BY THE TIME I'M OVERWHELMED!
SANDRA! COVER ME AS BEST YOU CAN WHILE I WORK MY WAY TOWARD YOU!
JOHN AND TARA! YOU'RE IN THE CLEAR, RUN! SEE IF YOU CAN SECURE A POINT OUTSIDE WE CAN ALL MEET UP AT--GET OUR ATTENTION AS YOU SEE US EXIT.

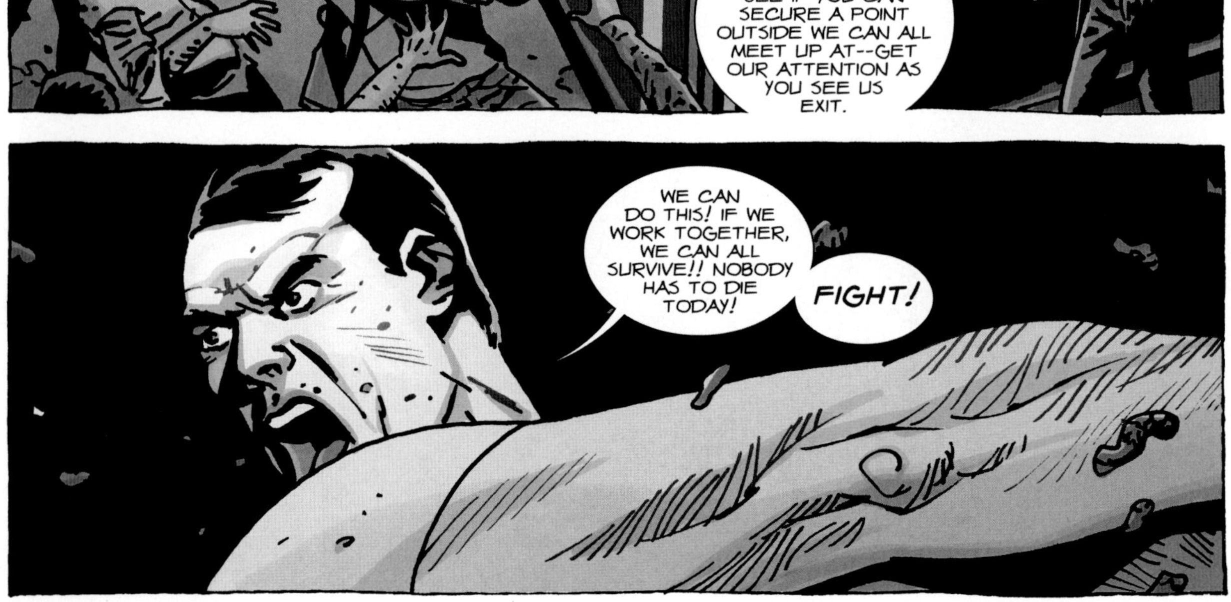
WE CAN DO THIS! IF WE WORK TOGETHER, WE CAN ALL SURVIVE!! NOBODY HAS TO DIE TODAY!
FIGHT!

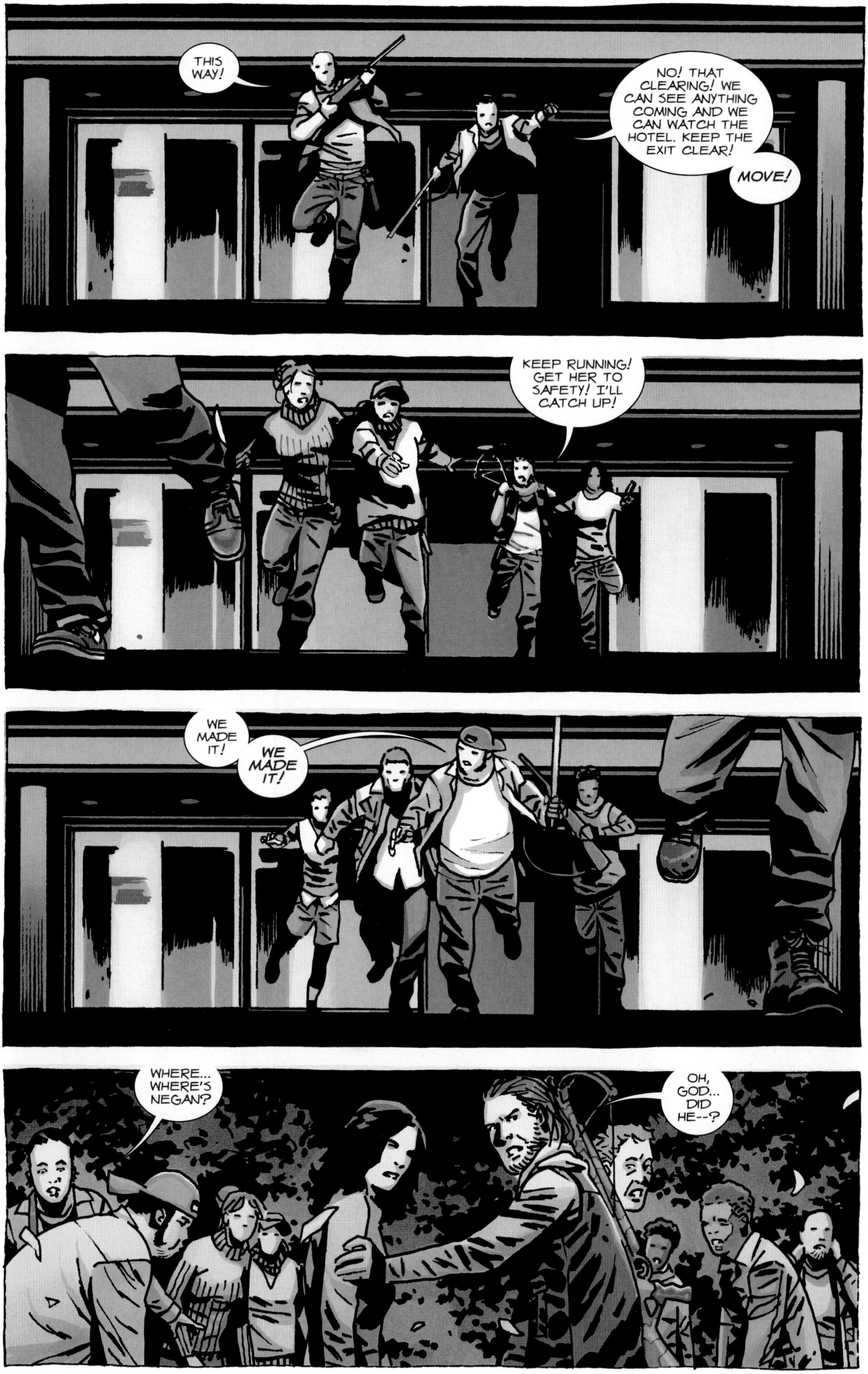
THIS WAY!
NO! THAT CLEARING! WE CAN SEE ANYTHING COMING AND WE CAN WATCH THE HOTEL. KEEP THE EXIT CLEAR!
MOVE!
KEEP RUNNING! GET HER TO SAFETY! I'LL CATCH UP!
WE MADE IT!
WE MADE IT!
WHERE... WHERE'S NEGAN?
OH, GOD... DID HE--?

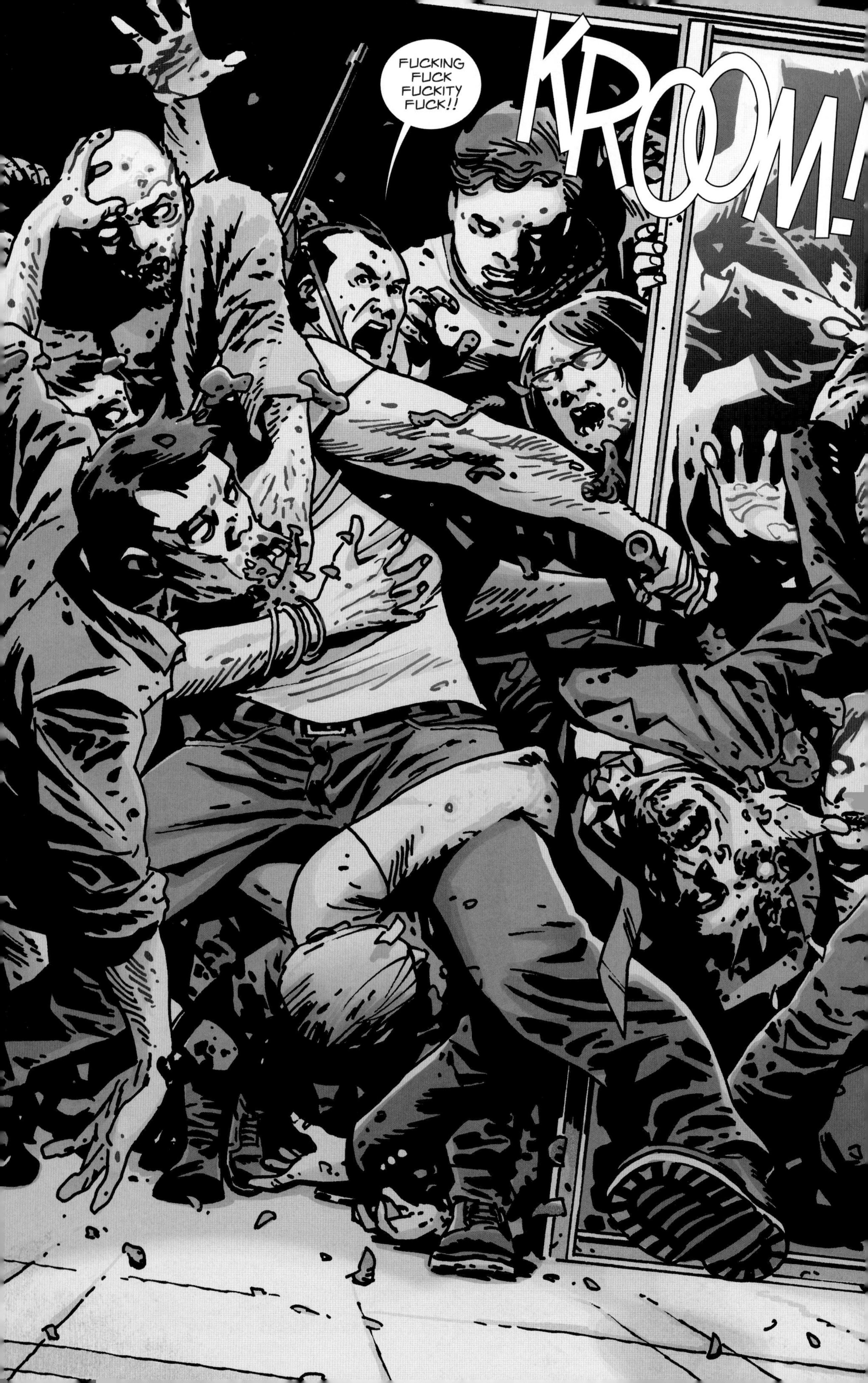
FUCKING FUCK FUCKITY FUCK!!
KROOOM!!

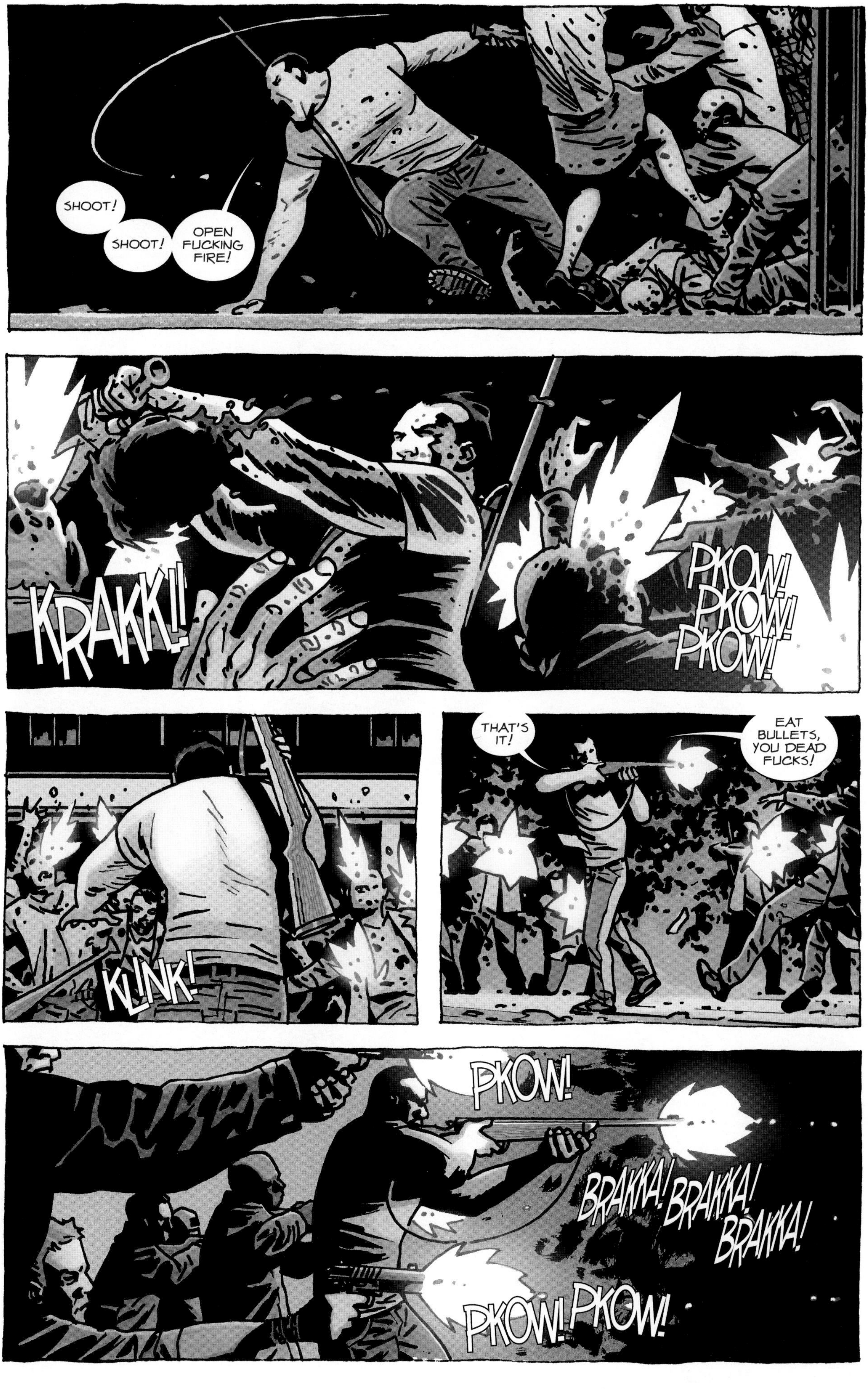
SHOOT!
SHOOT!
OPEN FUCKING FIRE!
KRAKK!!
PKOW! PKOW! PKOW!
KLINK!
THAT'S IT!
EAT BULLETS, YOU DEAD FUCKS!
PKOW!
BRAKKA! BRAKKA! BRAKKA!
PKOW! PKOW!

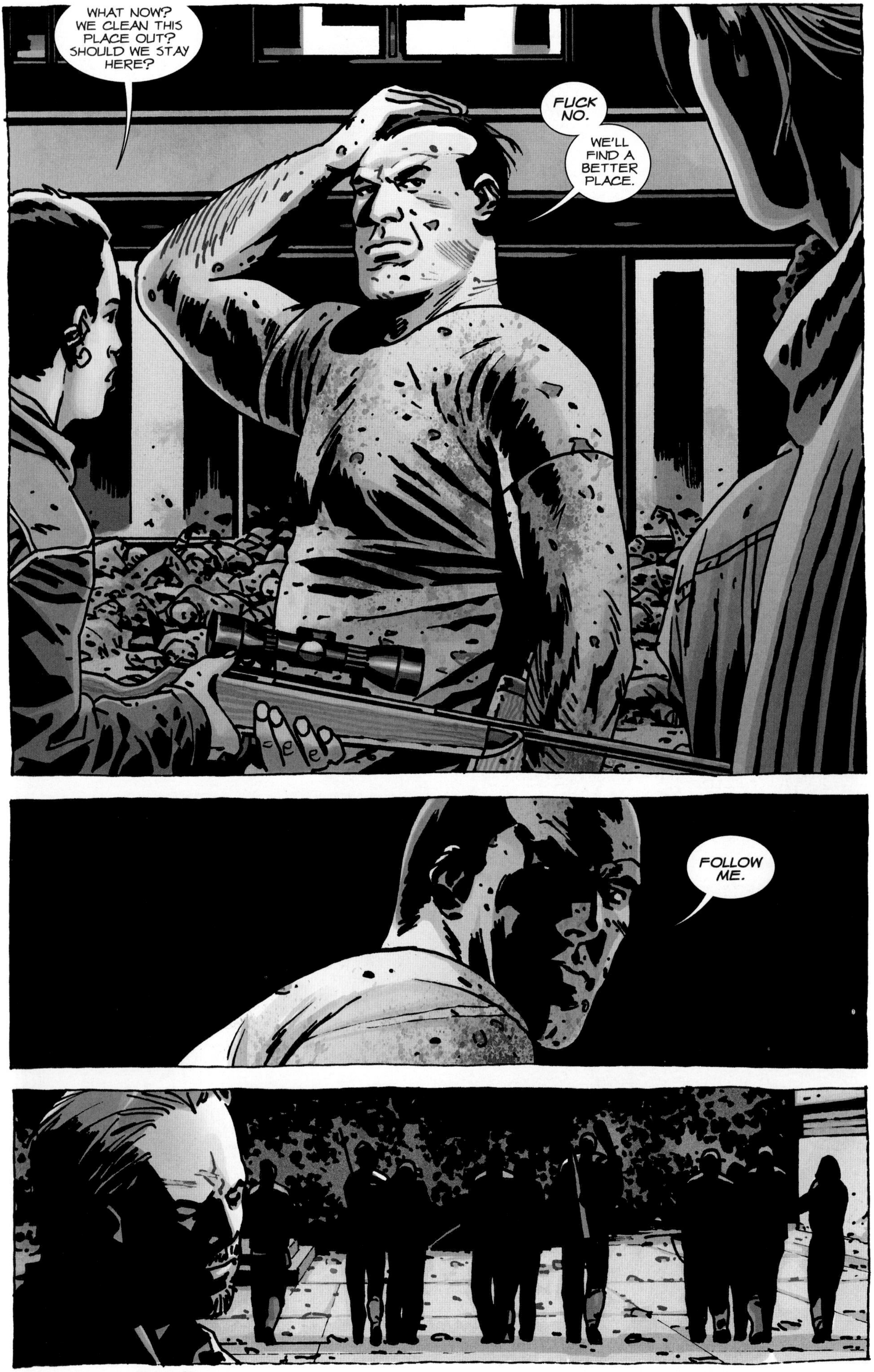
WHAT NOW? WE CLEAN THIS PLACE OUT? SHOULD WE STAY HERE?
FUCK NO.
WE'LL FIND A BETTER PLACE.
FOLLOW ME.

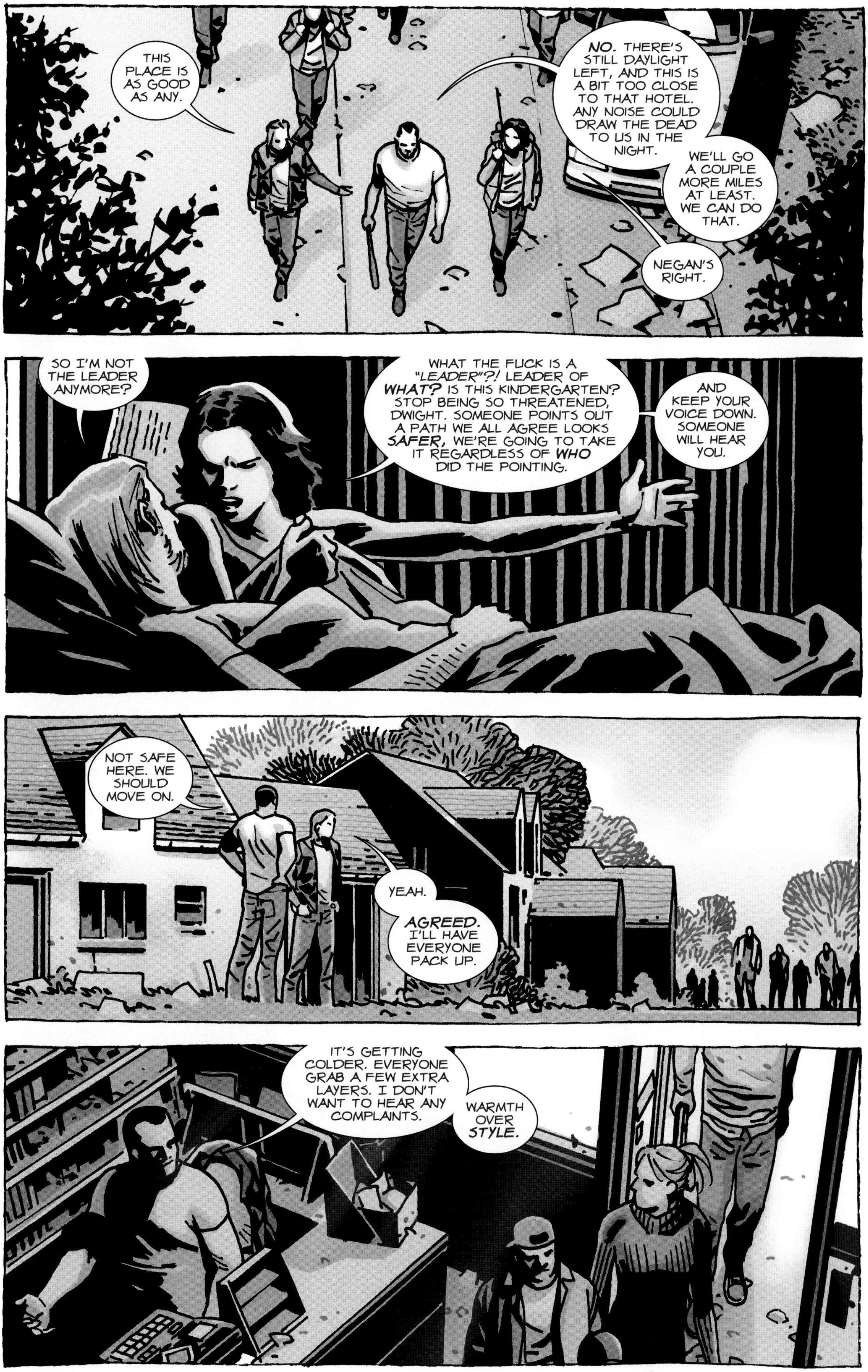
THIS PLACE IS AS GOOD AS ANY.
NO. THERE'S STILL DAYLIGHT LEFT, AND THIS IS A BIT TOO CLOSE TO THAT HOTEL. ANY NOISE COULD DRAW THE DEAD TO US IN THE NIGHT.
WE'LL GO A COUPLE MORE MILES AT LEAST. WE CAN DO THAT.
NEGAN'S RIGHT.
SO I'M NOT THE LEADER ANYMORE?
WHAT THE FUCK IS A "LEADER"?! LEADER OF WHAT? IS THIS KINDERGARTEN? STOP BEING SO THREATENED, DWIGHT. SOMEONE POINTS OUT A PATH WE ALL AGREE LOOKS SAFER, WE'RE GOING TO TAKE IT REGARDLESS OF WHO DID THE POINTING.
AND KEEP YOUR VOICE DOWN. SOMEONE WILL HEAR YOU.
NOT SAFE HERE. WE SHOULD MOVE ON.
YEAH.
AGREED. I'LL HAVE EVERYONE PACK UP.
IT'S GETTING COLDER. EVERYONE GRAB A FEW EXTRA LAYERS. I DON'T WANT TO HEAR ANY COMPLAINTS.
WARMTH OVER STYLE.

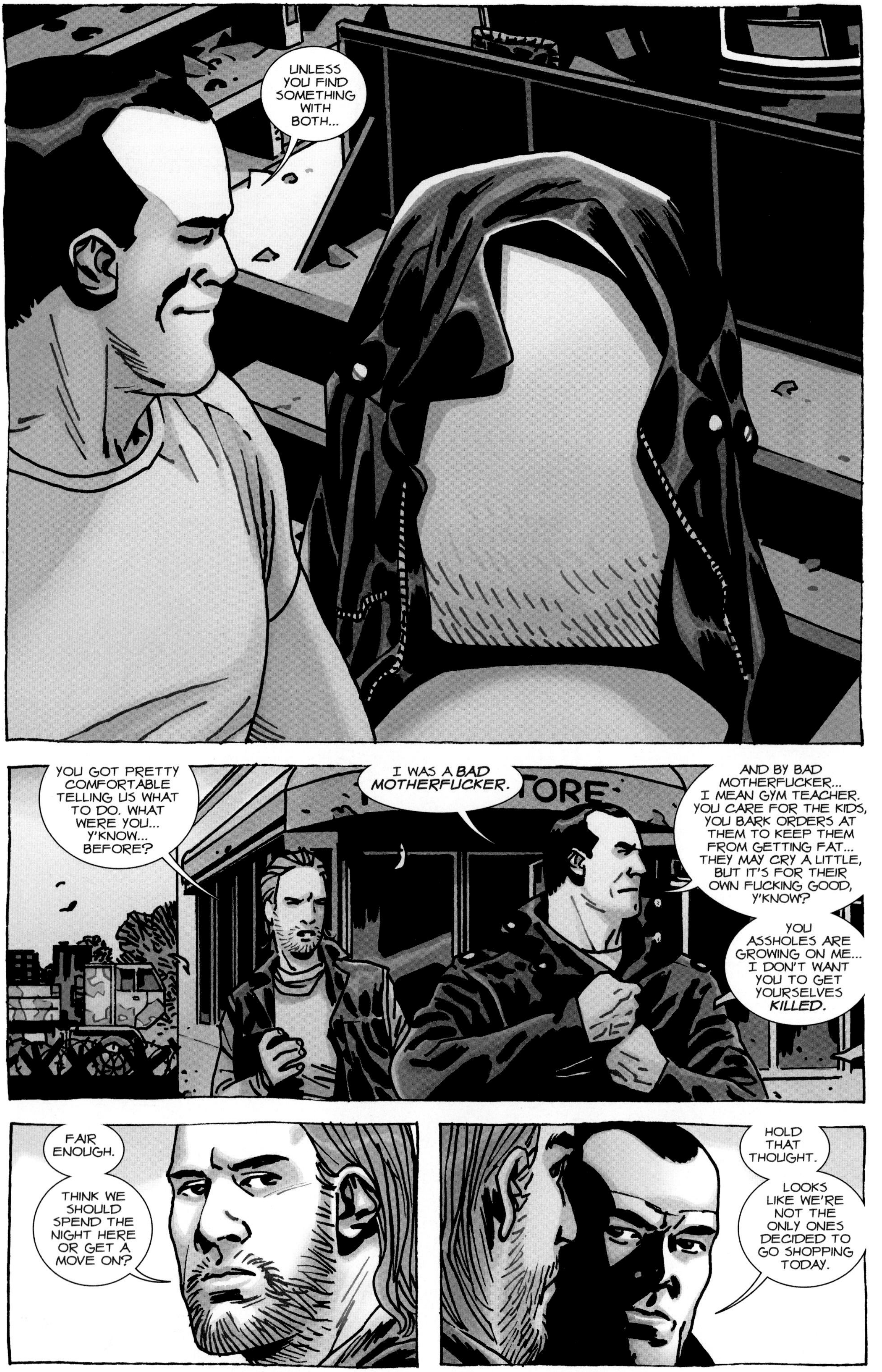
UNLESS YOU FIND SOMETHING WITH BOTH...
YOU GOT PRETTY COMFORTABLE TELLING US WHAT TO DO. WHAT WERE YOU... Y'KNOW... BEFORE?
I WAS A *BAD MOTHERFUCKER.*
AND BY BAD MOTHERFUCKER... I MEAN GYM TEACHER. YOU CARE FOR THE KIDS, YOU BARK ORDERS AT THEM TO KEEP THEM FROM GETTING FAT... THEY MAY CRY A LITTLE, BUT IT'S FOR THEIR OWN FUCKING GOOD, Y'KNOW?
YOU ASSHOLES ARE GROWING ON ME... I DON'T WANT YOU TO GET YOURSELVES ***KILLED.***
FAIR ENOUGH.
THINK WE SHOULD SPEND THE NIGHT HERE OR GET A MOVE ON?
HOLD THAT THOUGHT.
LOOKS LIKE WE'RE NOT THE ONLY ONES DECIDED TO GO SHOPPING TODAY.

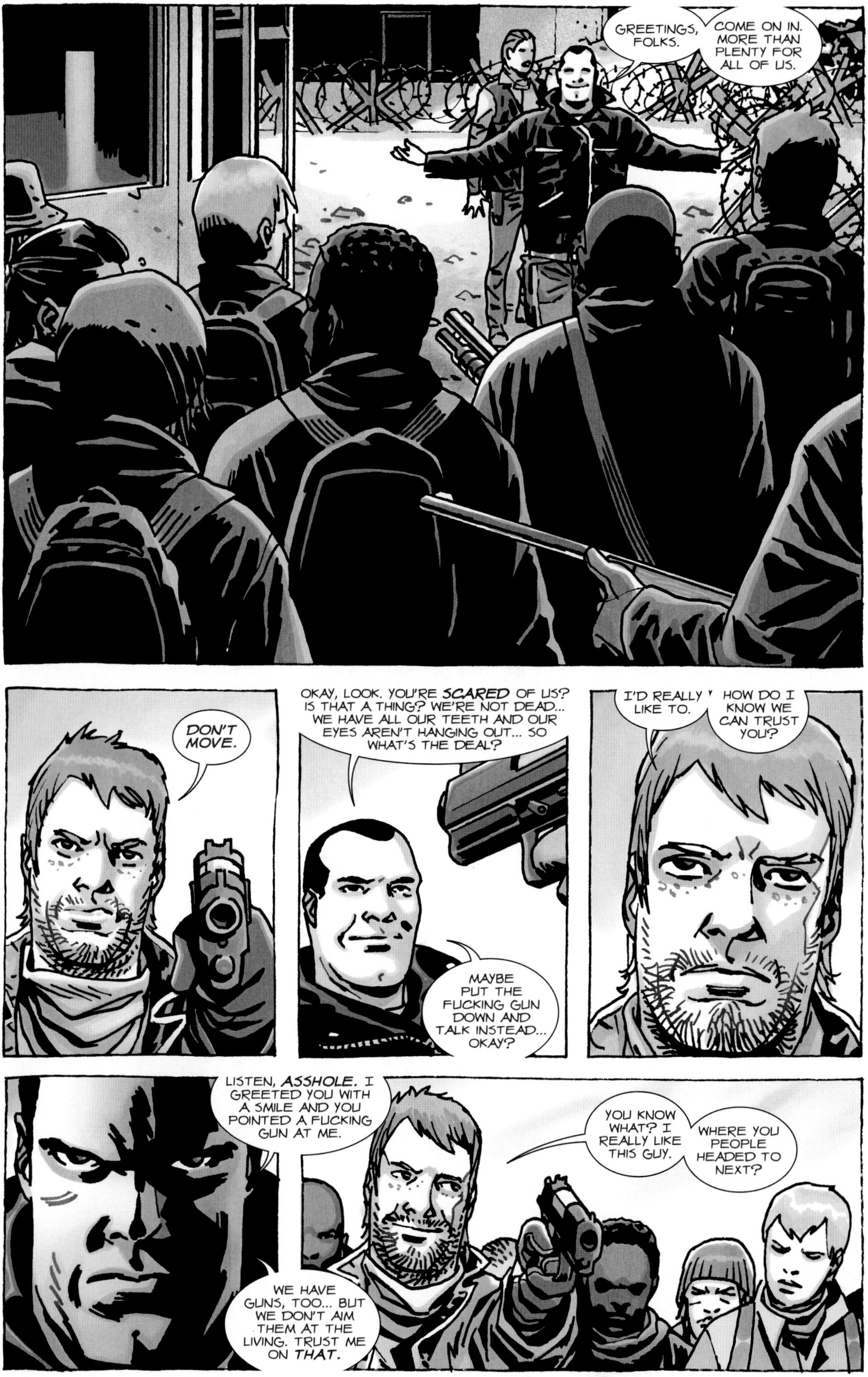
GREETINGS, FOLKS.
COME ON IN. MORE THAN PLENTY FOR ALL OF US.
DON'T MOVE.
OKAY, LOOK. YOU'RE SCARED OF US? IS THAT A THING? WE'RE NOT DEAD... WE HAVE ALL OUR TEETH AND OUR EYES AREN'T HANGING OUT... SO WHAT'S THE DEAL?
MAYBE PUT THE FUCKING GUN DOWN AND TALK INSTEAD... OKAY?
I'D REALLY LIKE TO.
HOW DO I KNOW WE CAN TRUST YOU?
LISTEN, ASSHOLE. I GREETED YOU WITH A SMILE AND YOU POINTED A FUCKING GUN AT ME.
WE HAVE GUNS, TOO... BUT WE DON'T AIM THEM AT THE LIVING. TRUST ME ON THAT.
YOU KNOW WHAT? I REALLY LIKE THIS GUY.
WHERE YOU PEOPLE HEADED TO NEXT?

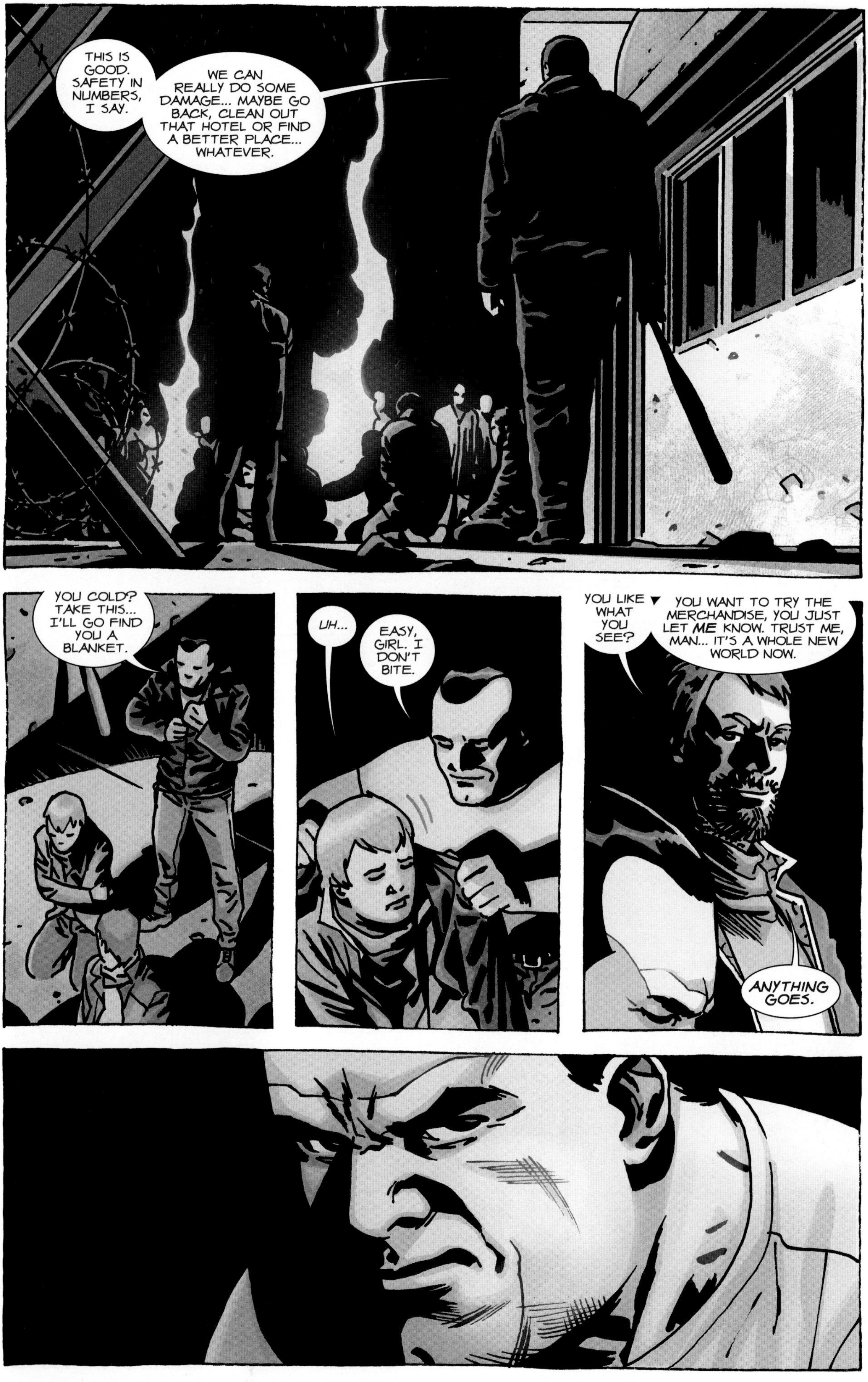
THIS IS GOOD. SAFETY IN NUMBERS, I SAY.
WE CAN REALLY DO SOME DAMAGE... MAYBE GO BACK, CLEAN OUT THAT HOTEL OR FIND A BETTER PLACE... WHATEVER.
YOU COLD? TAKE THIS... I'LL GO FIND YOU A BLANKET.
UH...
EASY, GIRL. I DON'T BITE.
YOU LIKE WHAT YOU SEE?
YOU WANT TO TRY THE MERCHANDISE, YOU JUST LET ME KNOW. TRUST ME, MAN... IT'S A WHOLE NEW WORLD NOW.
ANYTHING GOES.

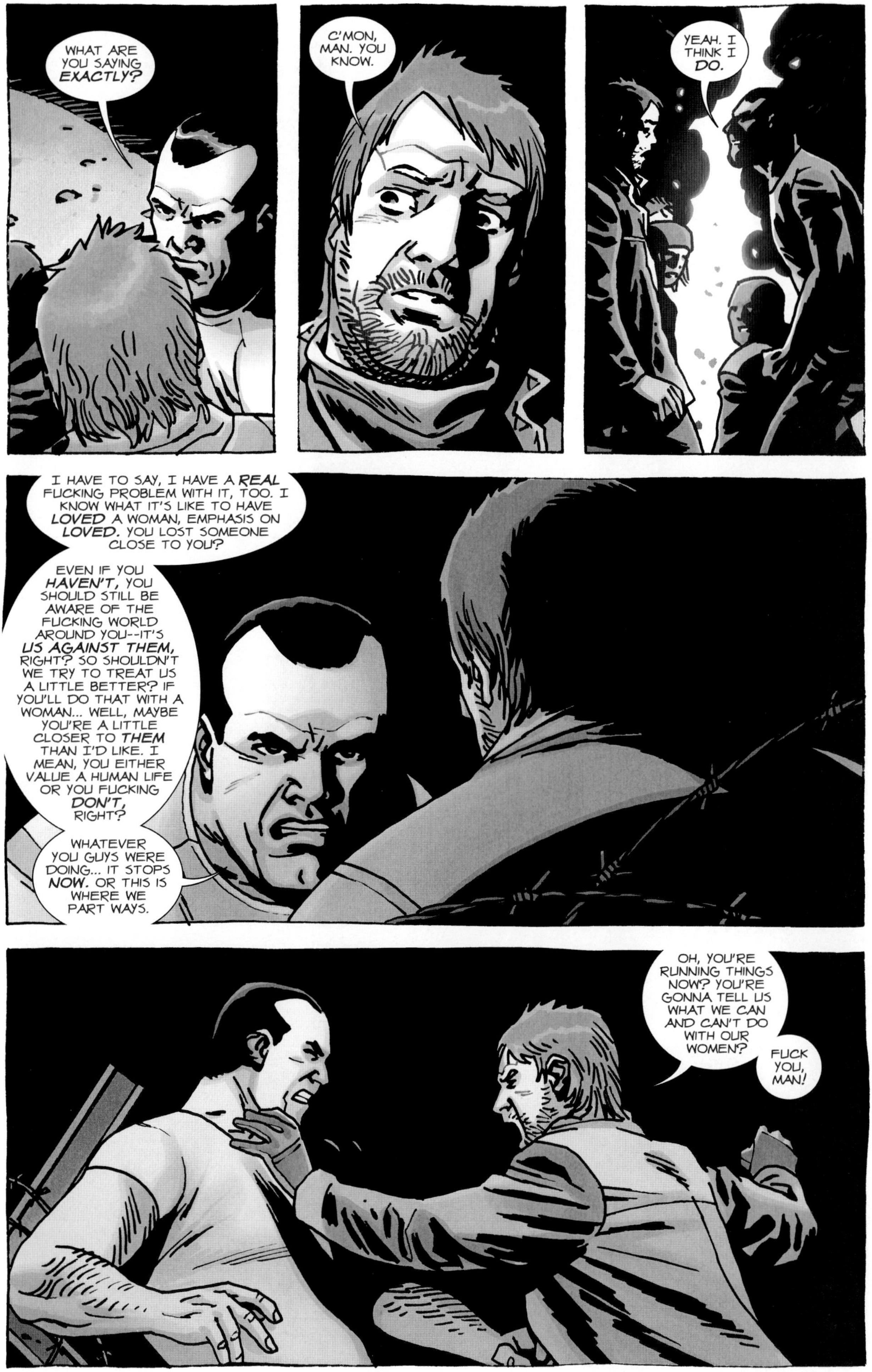

WHAT ARE YOU SAYING EXACTLY?
C'MON, MAN. YOU KNOW.
YEAH. I THINK I DO.
I HAVE TO SAY, I HAVE A REAL FUCKING PROBLEM WITH IT, TOO. I KNOW WHAT IT'S LIKE TO HAVE LOVED A WOMAN, EMPHASIS ON LOVED. YOU LOST SOMEONE CLOSE TO YOU?
EVEN IF YOU HAVEN'T, YOU SHOULD STILL BE AWARE OF THE FUCKING WORLD AROUND YOU--IT'S US AGAINST THEM, RIGHT? SO SHOULDN'T WE TRY TO TREAT US A LITTLE BETTER? IF YOU'LL DO THAT WITH A WOMAN... WELL, MAYBE YOU'RE A LITTLE CLOSER TO THEM THAN I'D LIKE. I MEAN, YOU EITHER VALUE A HUMAN LIFE OR YOU FUCKING DON'T, RIGHT?
WHATEVER YOU GUYS WERE DOING... IT STOPS NOW. OR THIS IS WHERE WE PART WAYS.
OH, YOU'RE RUNNING THINGS NOW? YOU'RE GONNA TELL US WHAT WE CAN AND CAN'T DO WITH OUR WOMEN?
FUCK YOU, MAN!

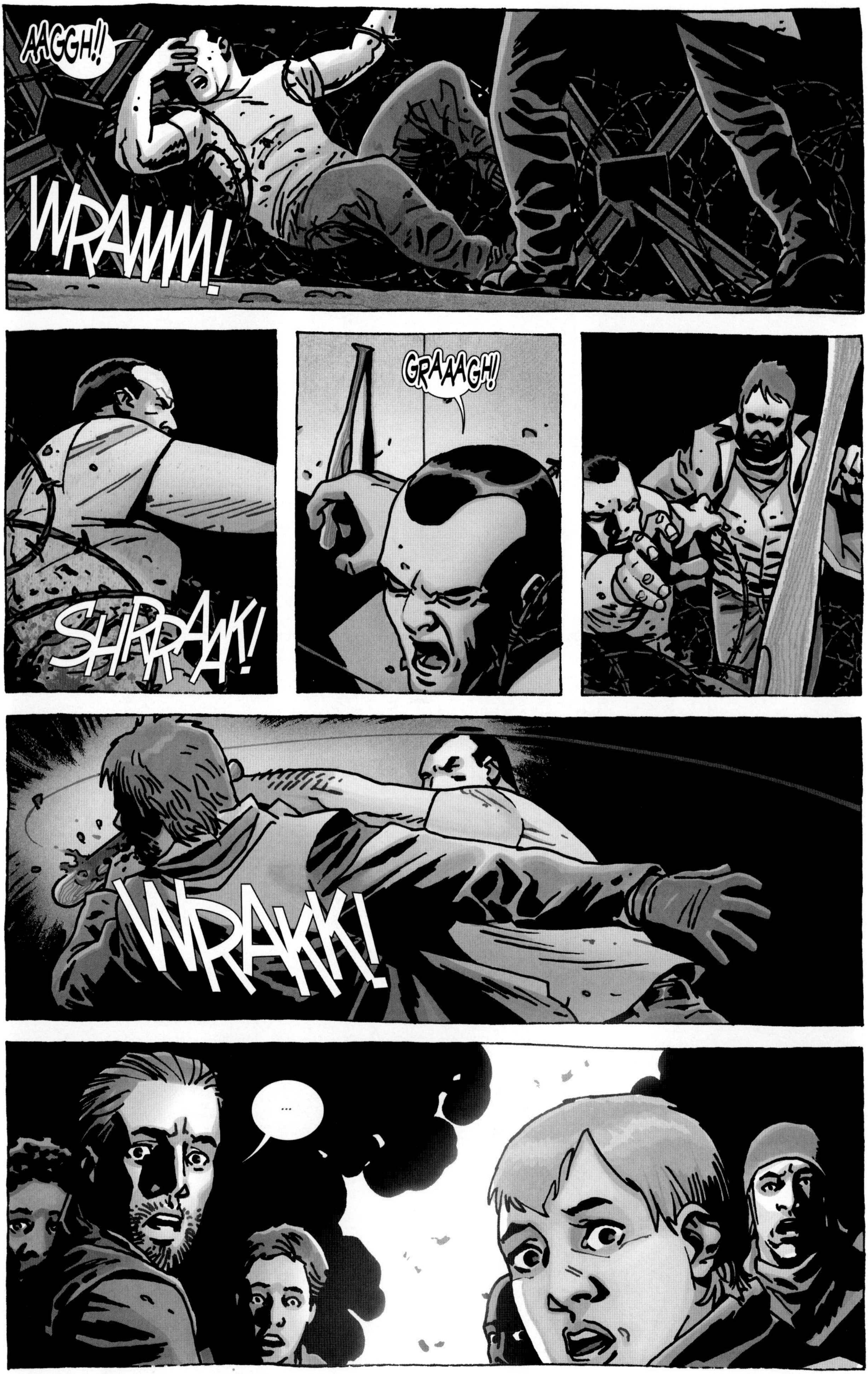
AAGGH!!
WRAMM!
SHRRAAK!
GRAAAGH!
WRAKK!
...

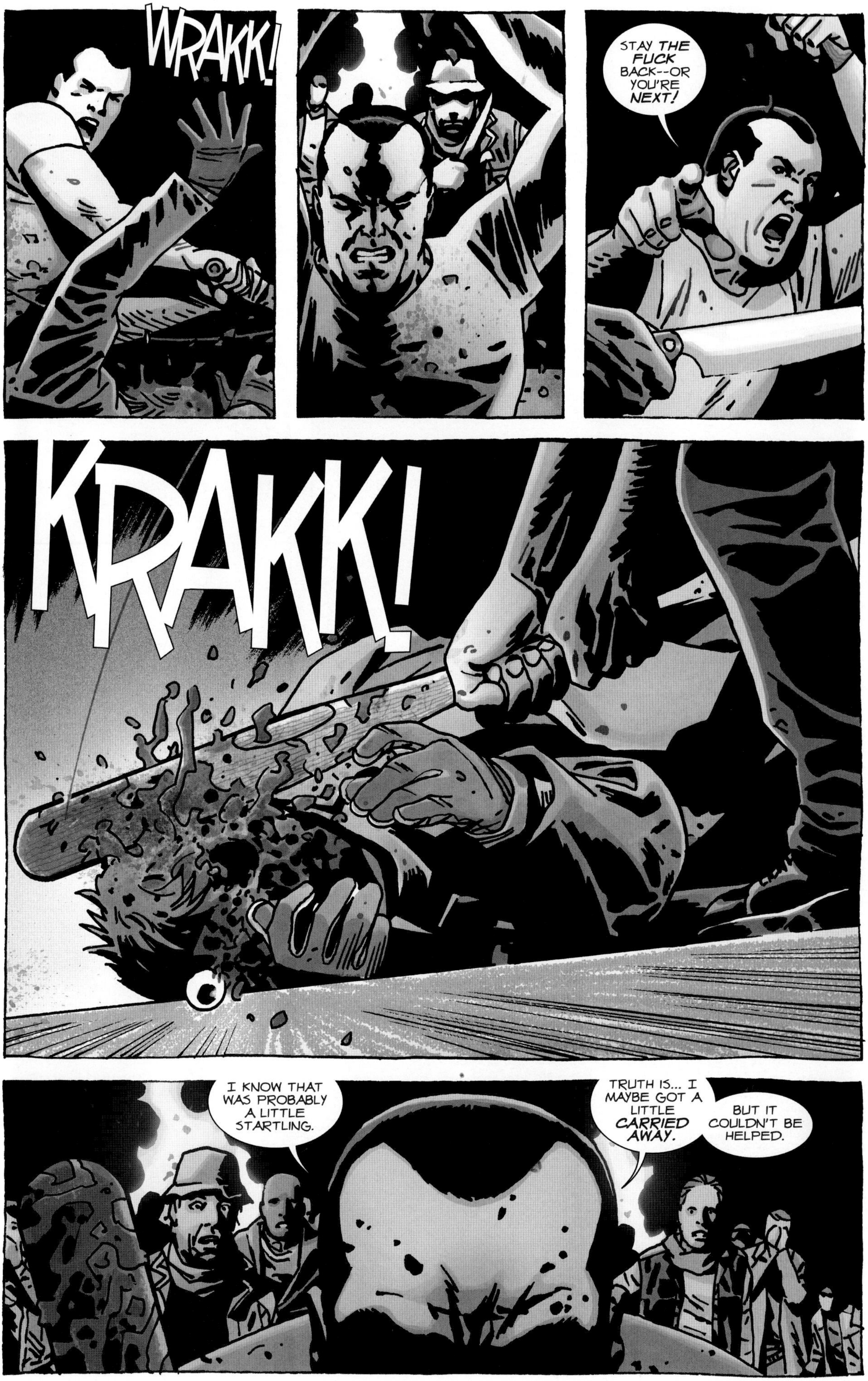
WRAKK!
STAY THE FUCK BACK--OR YOU'RE NEXT!
KRAKK!
I KNOW THAT WAS PROBABLY A LITTLE STARTLING.
TRUTH IS... I MAYBE GOT A LITTLE CARRIED AWAY.
BUT IT COULDN'T BE HELPED.

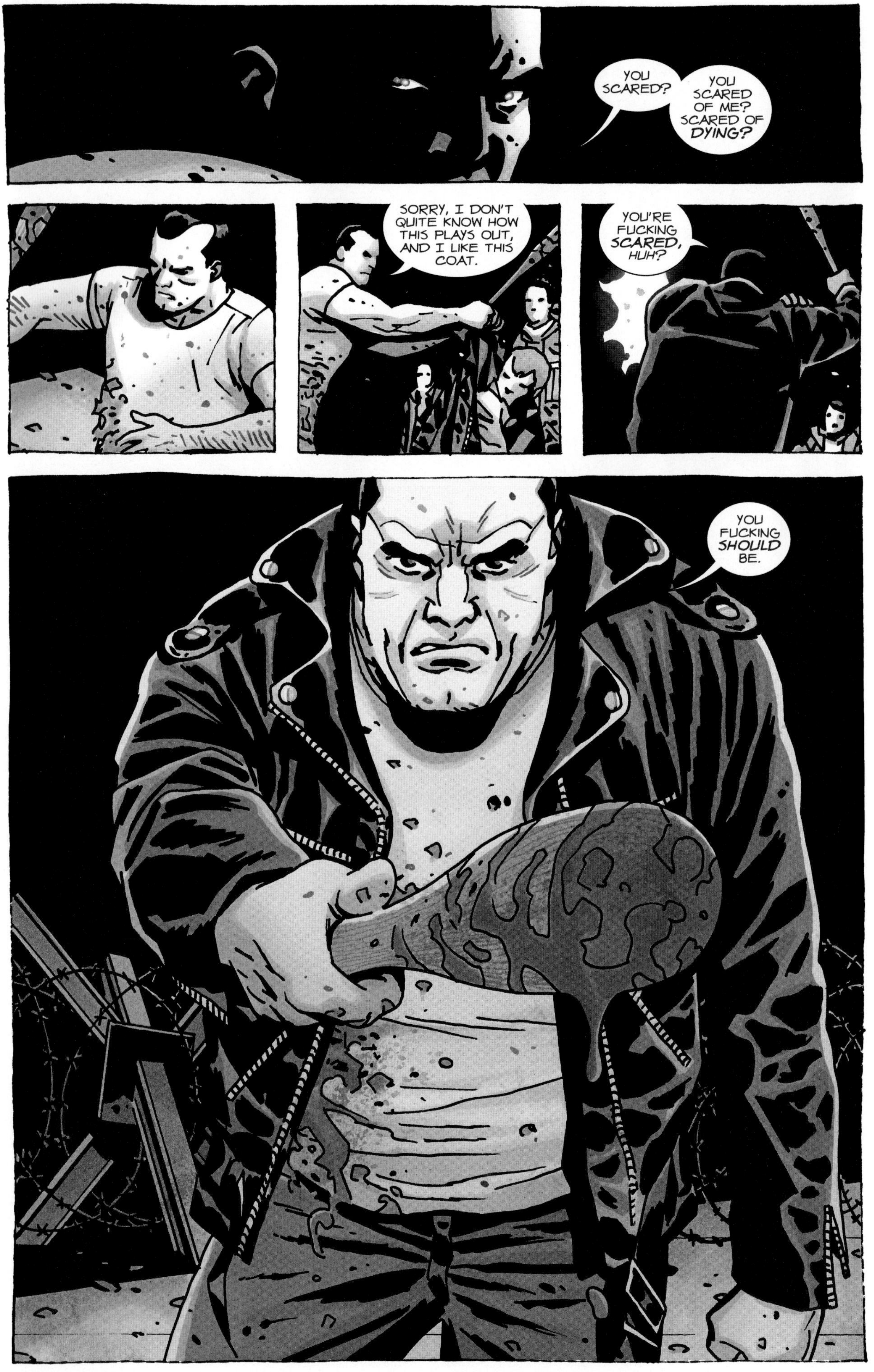

YOU SCARED?
YOU SCARED OF ME? SCARED OF DYING?
SORRY, I DON'T QUITE KNOW HOW THIS PLAYS OUT, AND I LIKE THIS COAT.
YOU'RE FUCKING SCARED, HUH?
YOU FUCKING SHOULD BE.

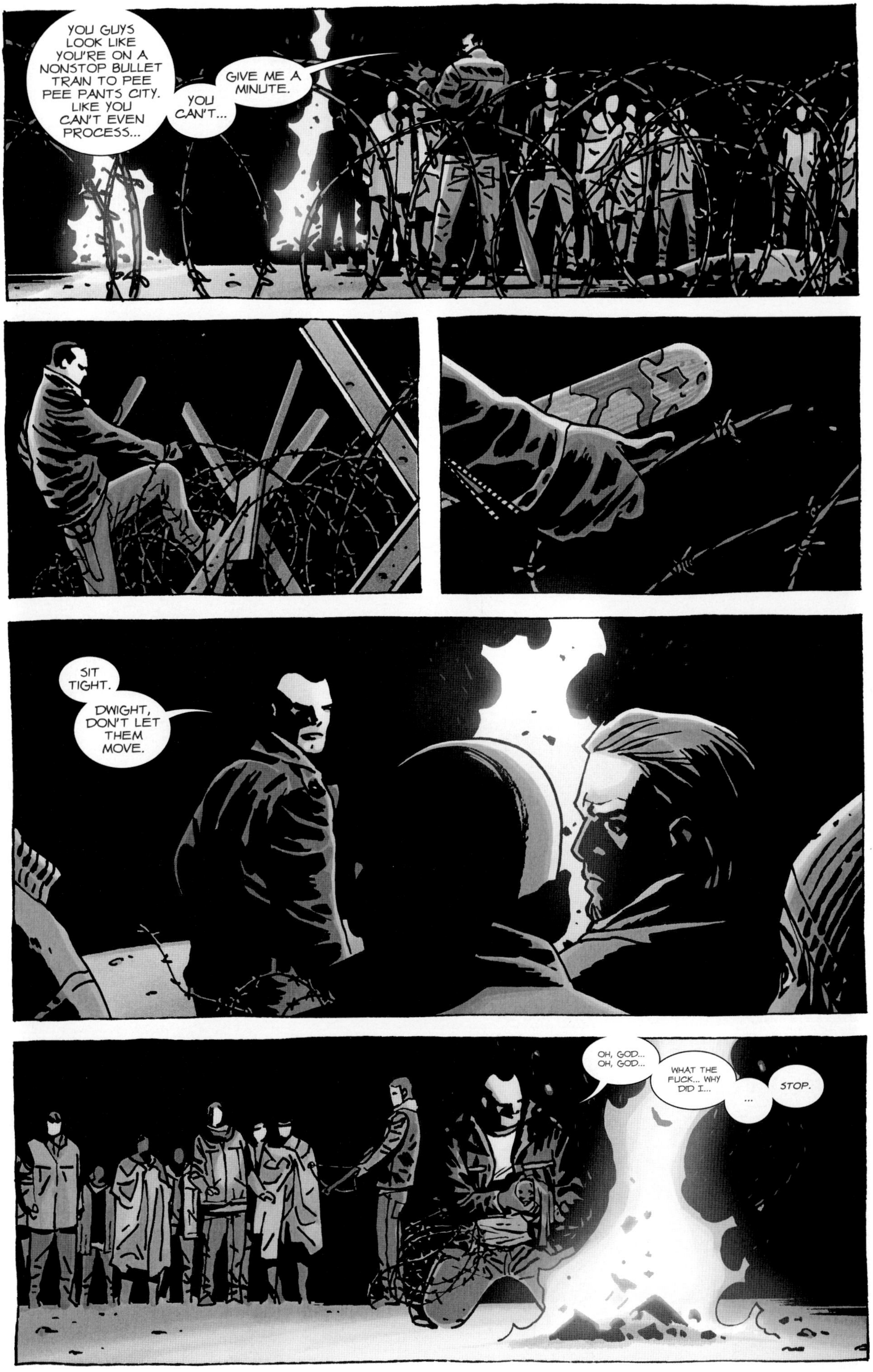
YOU GUYS LOOK LIKE YOU'RE ON A NONSTOP BULLET TRAIN TO PEE PEE PANTS CITY. LIKE YOU CAN'T EVEN PROCESS...
YOU CAN'T...
GIVE ME A MINUTE.
SIT TIGHT.
DWIGHT, DON'T LET THEM MOVE.
OH, GOD... OH, GOD...
WHAT THE FUCK... WHY DID I...
...
STOP.

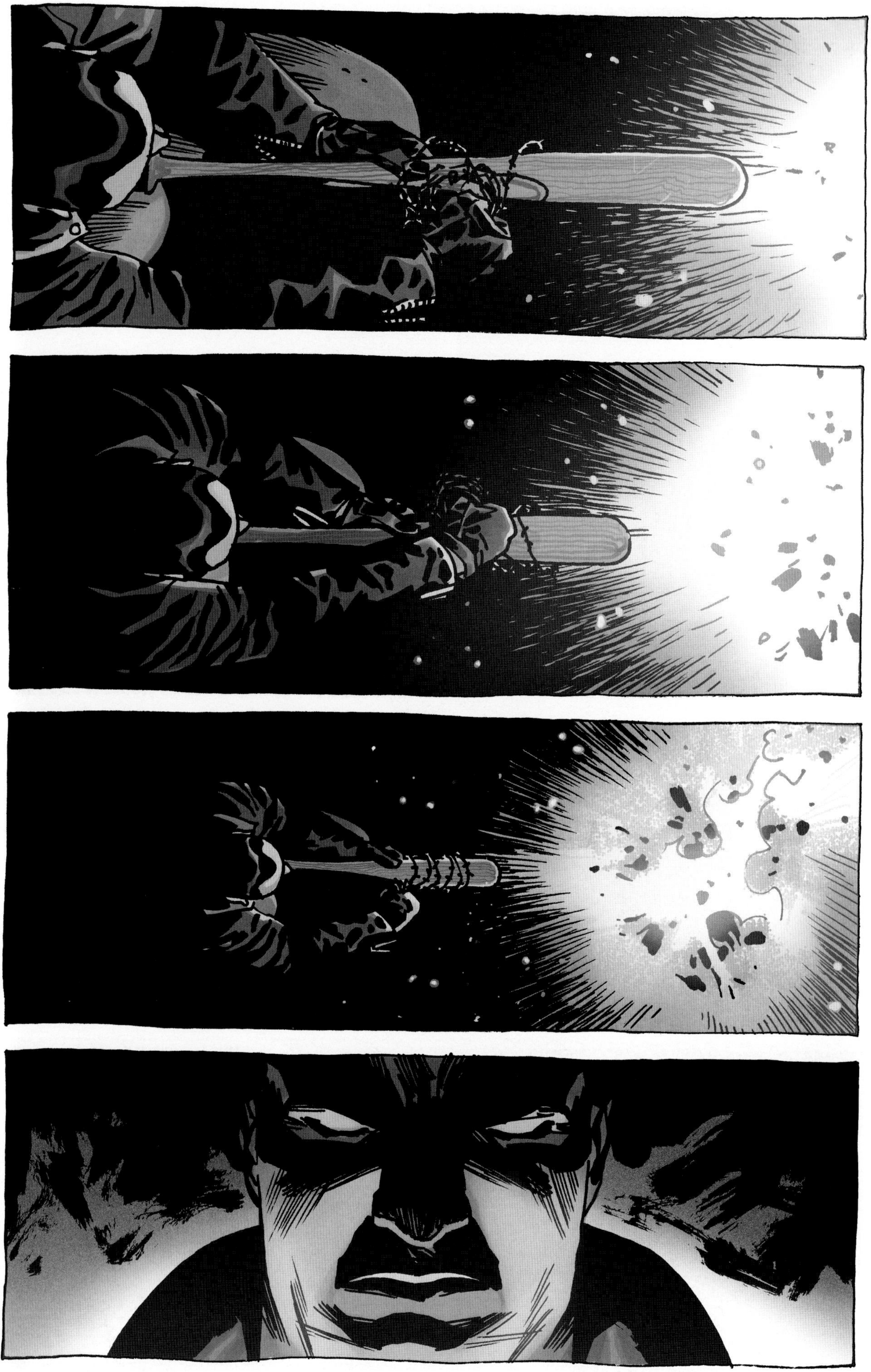

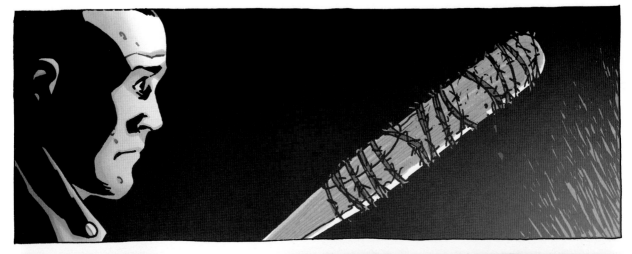

≥SIGH.≤

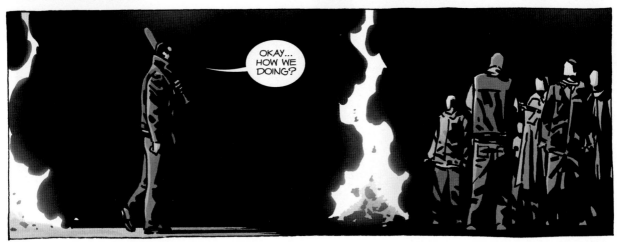

OKAY... HOW WE DOING?

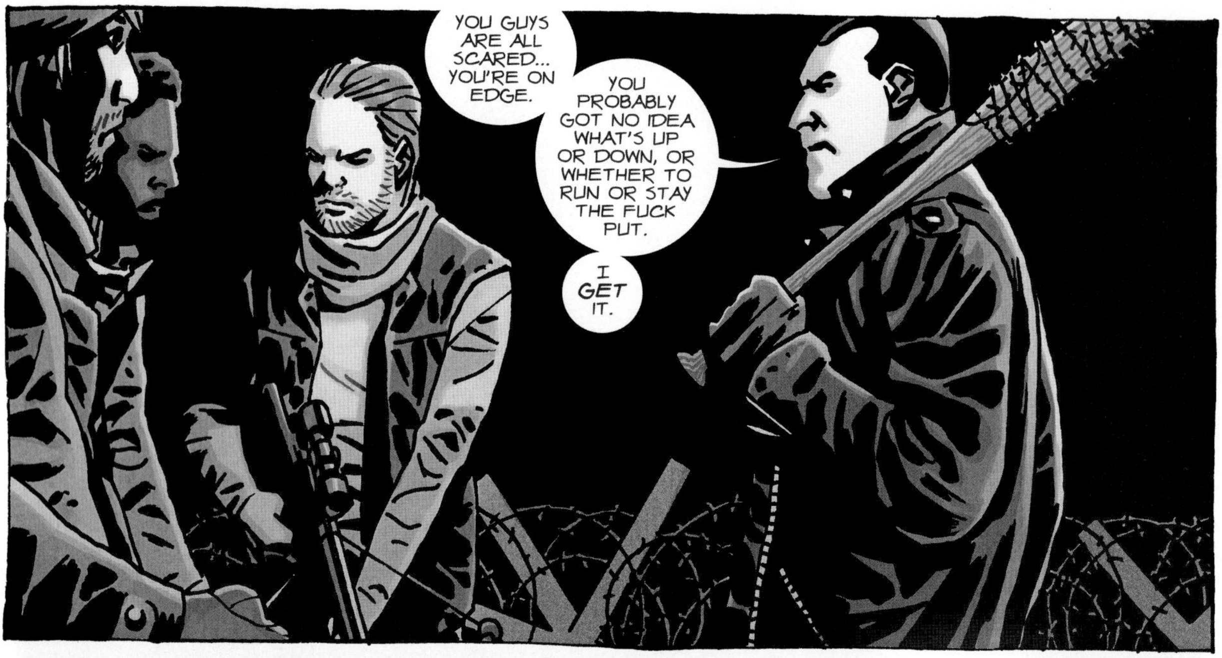
YOU GUYS ARE ALL SCARED... YOU'RE ON EDGE.
YOU PROBABLY GOT NO IDEA WHAT'S UP OR DOWN, OR WHETHER TO RUN OR STAY THE FUCK PUT.
I GET IT.

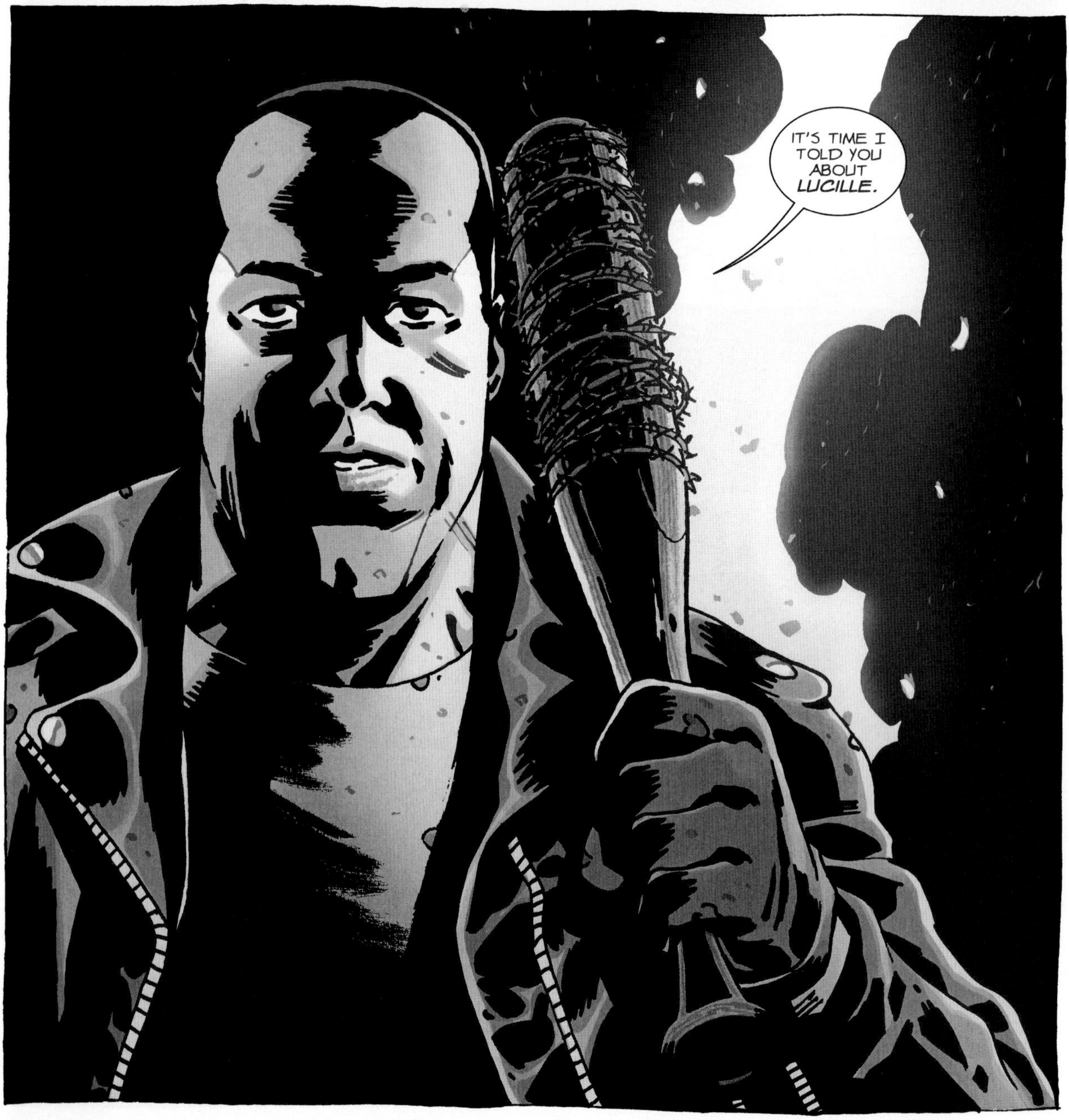
IT'S TIME I TOLD YOU ABOUT LUCILLE.

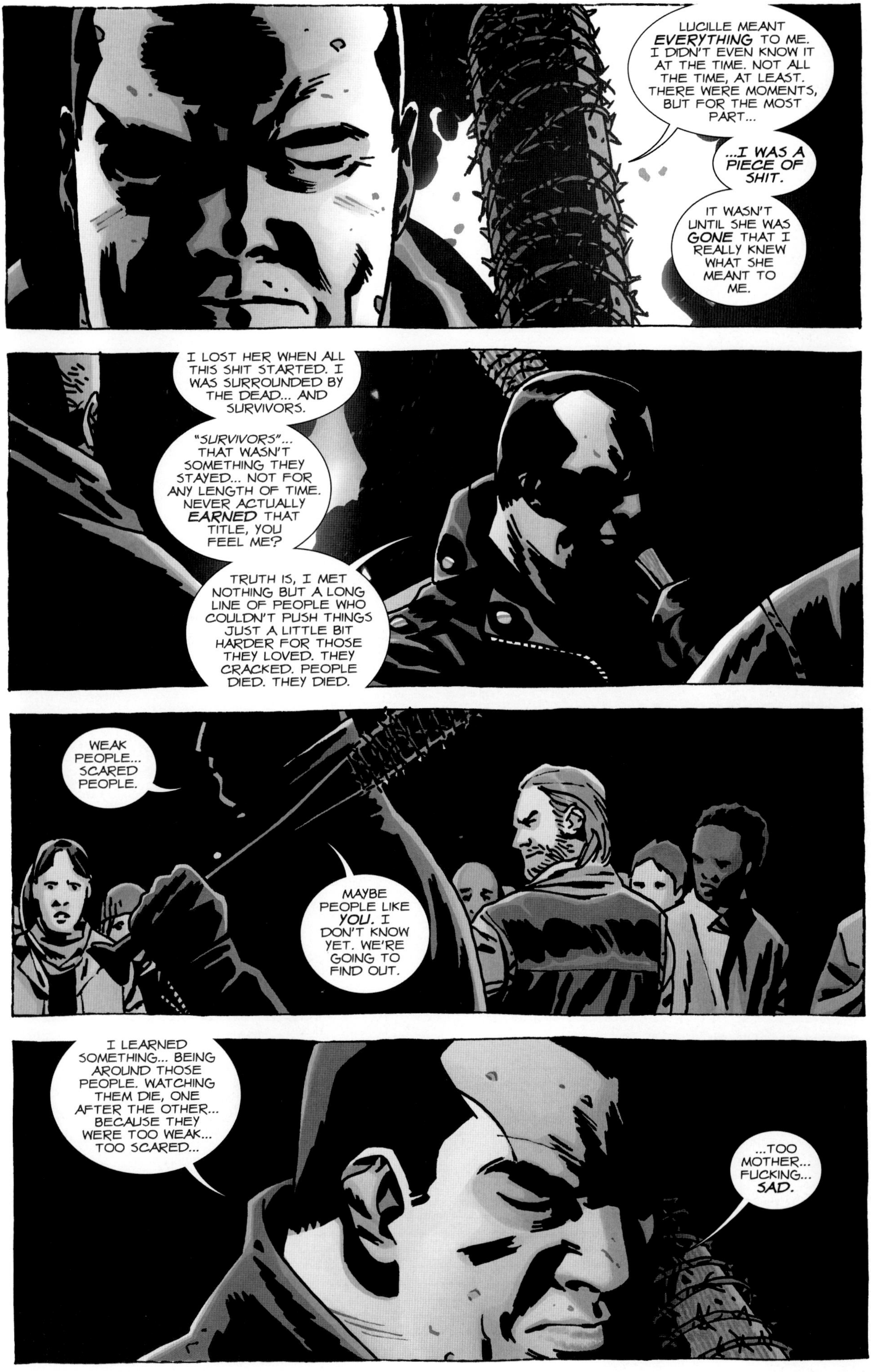
LUCILLE MEANT EVERYTHING TO ME. I DIDN'T EVEN KNOW IT AT THE TIME. NOT ALL THE TIME, AT LEAST. THERE WERE MOMENTS, BUT FOR THE MOST PART...
...I WAS A PIECE OF SHIT.
IT WASN'T UNTIL SHE WAS GONE THAT I REALLY KNEW WHAT SHE MEANT TO ME.
I LOST HER WHEN ALL THIS SHIT STARTED. I WAS SURROUNDED BY THE DEAD... AND SURVIVORS.
"SURVIVORS"... THAT WASN'T SOMETHING THEY STAYED... NOT FOR ANY LENGTH OF TIME. NEVER ACTUALLY EARNED THAT TITLE, YOU FEEL ME?
TRUTH IS, I MET NOTHING BUT A LONG LINE OF PEOPLE WHO COULDN'T PUSH THINGS JUST A LITTLE BIT HARDER FOR THOSE THEY LOVED. THEY CRACKED. PEOPLE DIED. THEY DIED.
WEAK PEOPLE... SCARED PEOPLE.
MAYBE PEOPLE LIKE YOU. I DON'T KNOW YET. WE'RE GOING TO FIND OUT.
I LEARNED SOMETHING... BEING AROUND THOSE PEOPLE. WATCHING THEM DIE, ONE AFTER THE OTHER... BECAUSE THEY WERE TOO WEAK... TOO SCARED...
...TOO MOTHER... FUCKING... SAD.

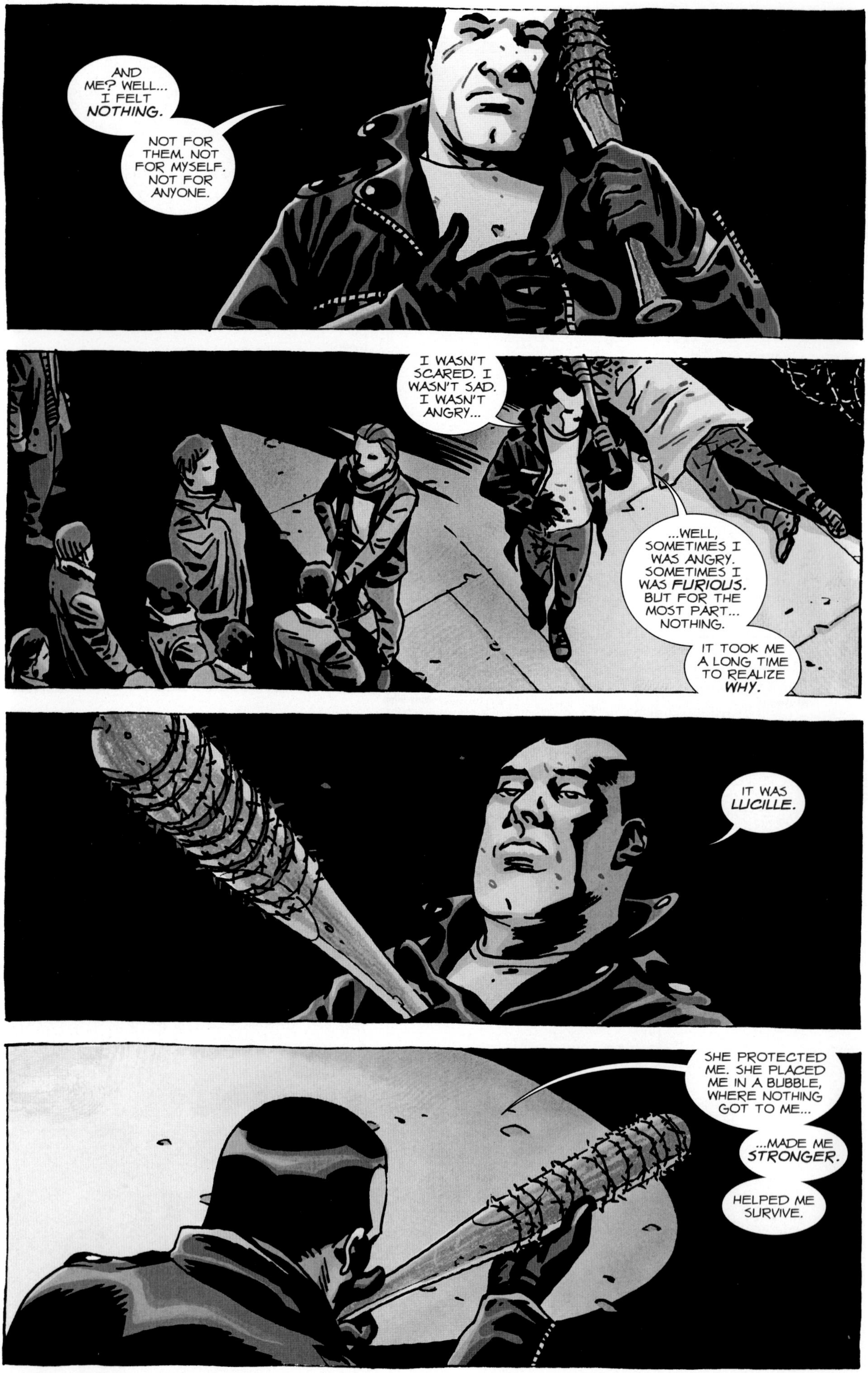
AND ME? WELL... I FELT NOTHING.
NOT FOR THEM. NOT FOR MYSELF. NOT FOR ANYONE.
I WASN'T SCARED. I WASN'T SAD. I WASN'T ANGRY...
...WELL, SOMETIMES I WAS ANGRY. SOMETIMES I WAS FURIOUS. BUT FOR THE MOST PART... NOTHING.
IT TOOK ME A LONG TIME TO REALIZE WHY.
IT WAS LUCILLE.
SHE PROTECTED ME. SHE PLACED ME IN A BUBBLE, WHERE NOTHING GOT TO ME...
...MADE ME STRONGER.
HELPED ME SURVIVE.

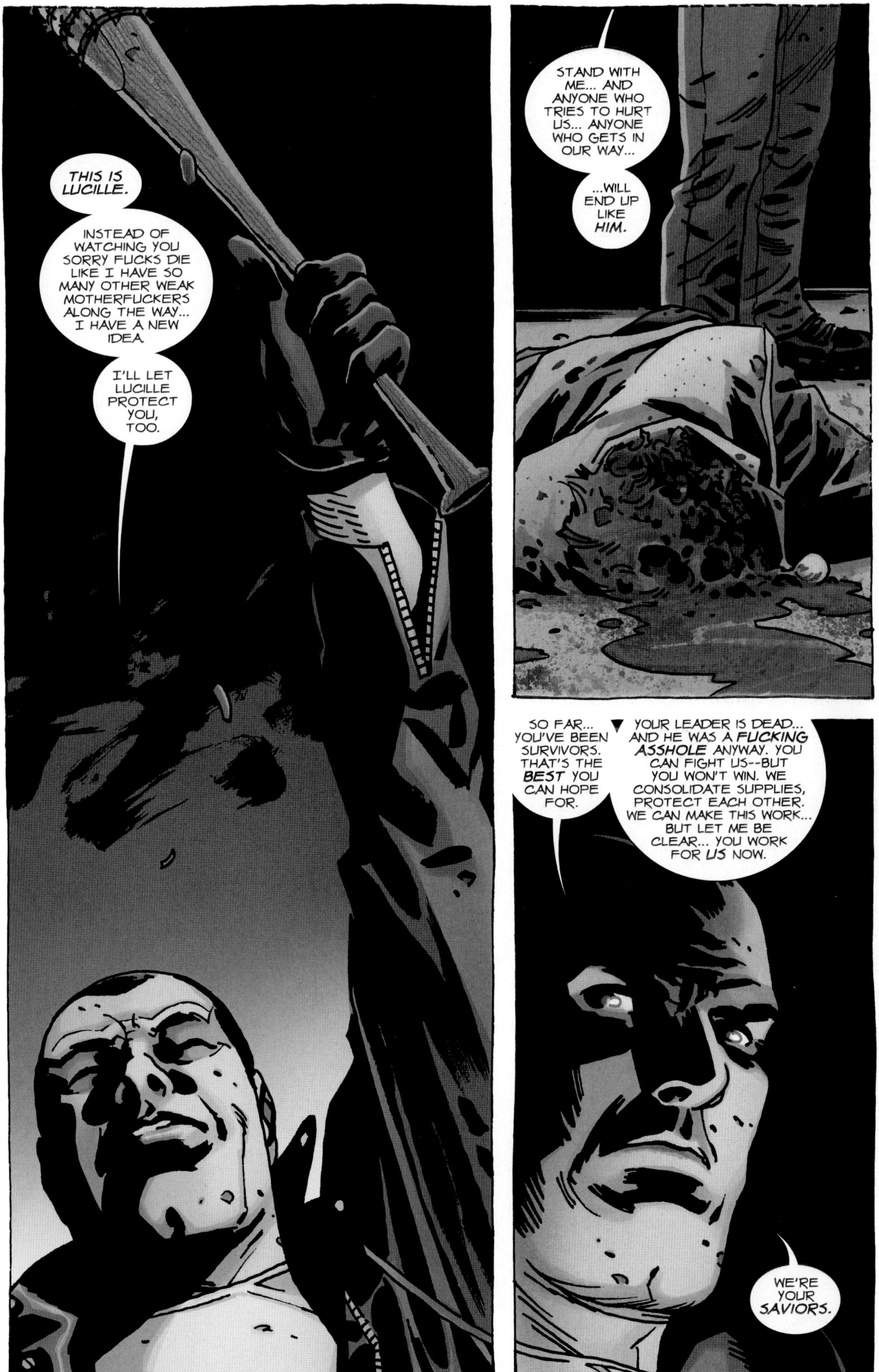
THIS IS LUCILLE.
INSTEAD OF WATCHING YOU SORRY FUCKS DIE LIKE I HAVE SO MANY OTHER WEAK MOTHERFUCKERS ALONG THE WAY... I HAVE A NEW IDEA.
I'LL LET LUCILLE PROTECT YOU, TOO.
STAND WITH ME... AND ANYONE WHO TRIES TO HURT US... ANYONE WHO GETS IN OUR WAY...
...WILL END UP LIKE HIM.
SO FAR... YOU'VE BEEN SURVIVORS. THAT'S THE BEST YOU CAN HOPE FOR.
YOUR LEADER IS DEAD... AND HE WAS A FUCKING ASSHOLE ANYWAY. YOU CAN FIGHT US--BUT YOU WON'T WIN. WE CONSOLIDATE SUPPLIES, PROTECT EACH OTHER. WE CAN MAKE THIS WORK... BUT LET ME BE CLEAR... YOU WORK FOR US NOW.
WE'RE YOUR SAVIORS.

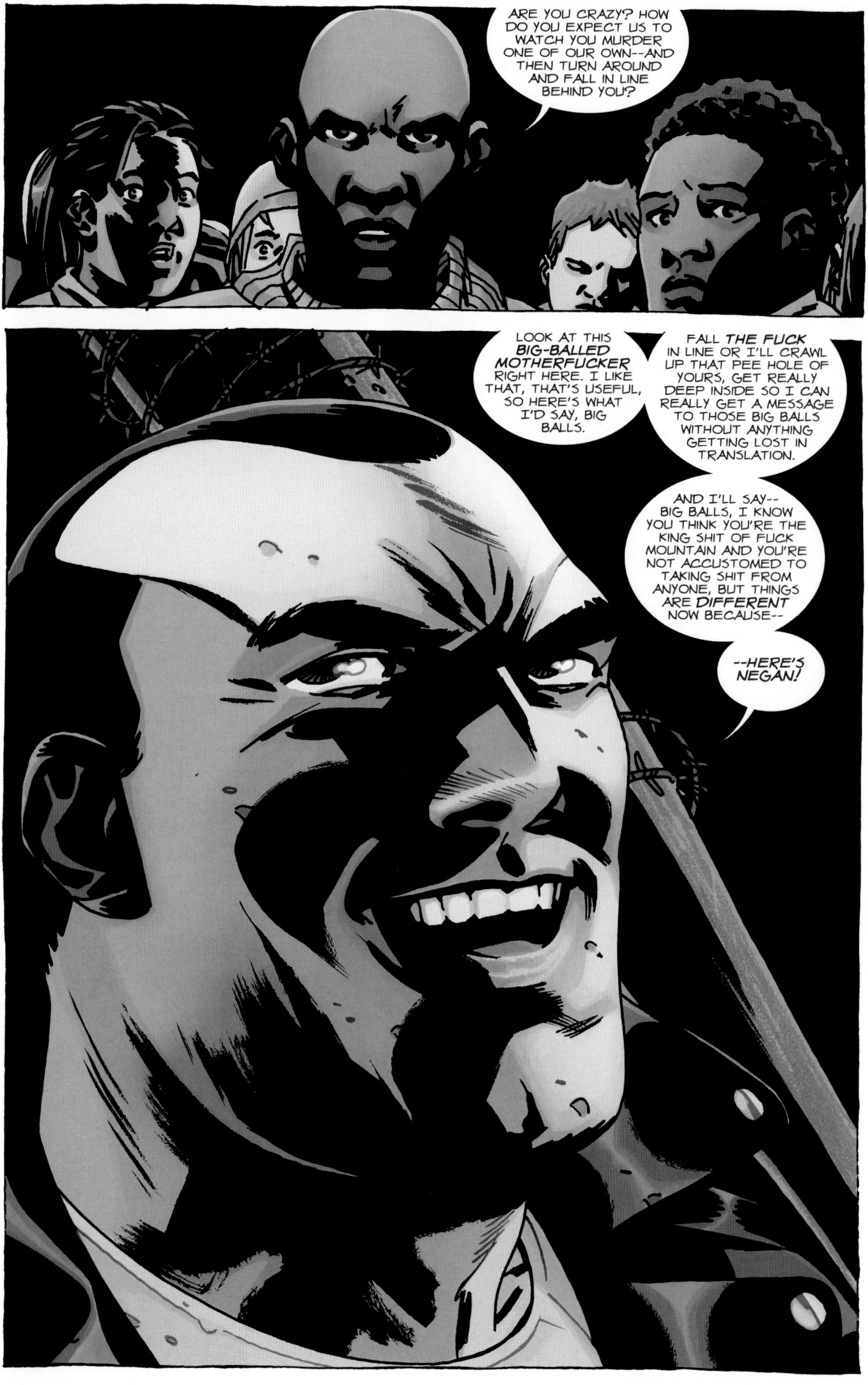
ARE YOU CRAZY? HOW DO YOU EXPECT US TO WATCH YOU MURDER ONE OF OUR OWN--AND THEN TURN AROUND AND FALL IN LINE BEHIND YOU?
LOOK AT THIS BIG-BALLED MOTHERFUCKER RIGHT HERE. I LIKE THAT, THAT'S USEFUL, SO HERE'S WHAT I'D SAY, BIG BALLS.
FALL THE FUCK IN LINE OR I'LL CRAWL UP THAT PEE HOLE OF YOURS, GET REALLY DEEP INSIDE SO I CAN REALLY GET A MESSAGE TO THOSE BIG BALLS WITHOUT ANYTHING GETTING LOST IN TRANSLATION.
AND I'LL SAY-- BIG BALLS, I KNOW YOU THINK YOU'RE THE KING SHIT OF FUCK MOUNTAIN AND YOU'RE NOT ACCUSTOMED TO TAKING SHIT FROM ANYONE, BUT THINGS ARE DIFFERENT NOW BECAUSE--
--HERE'S NEGAN!

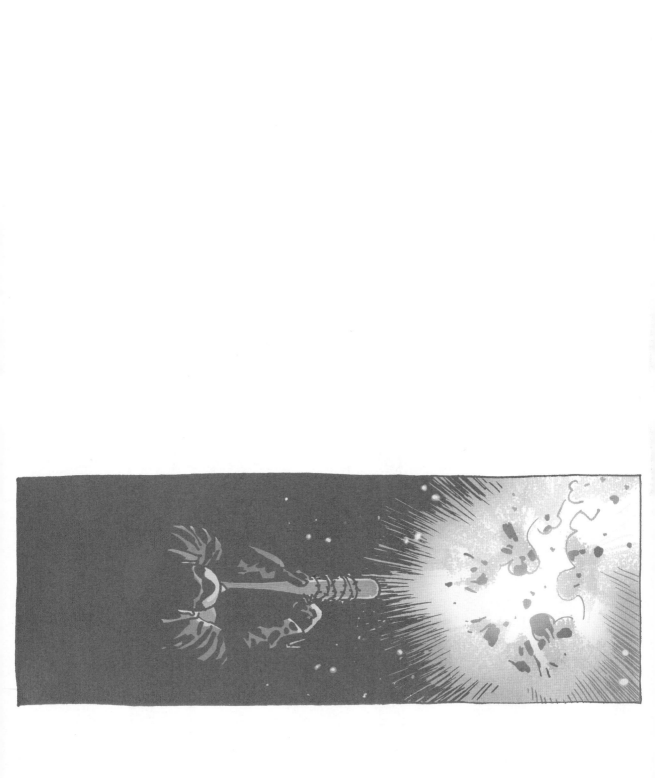

"It's time I told you about...

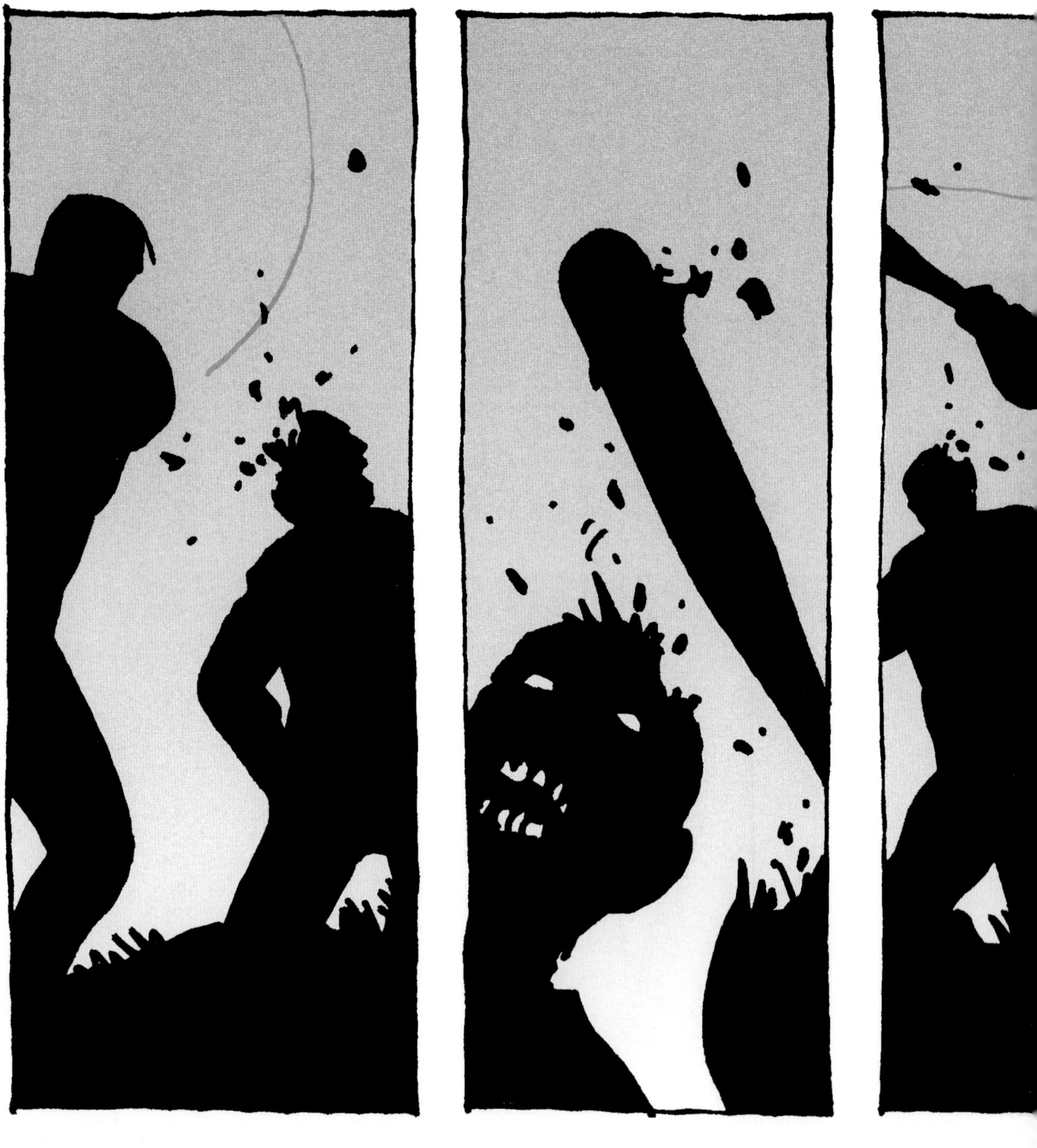

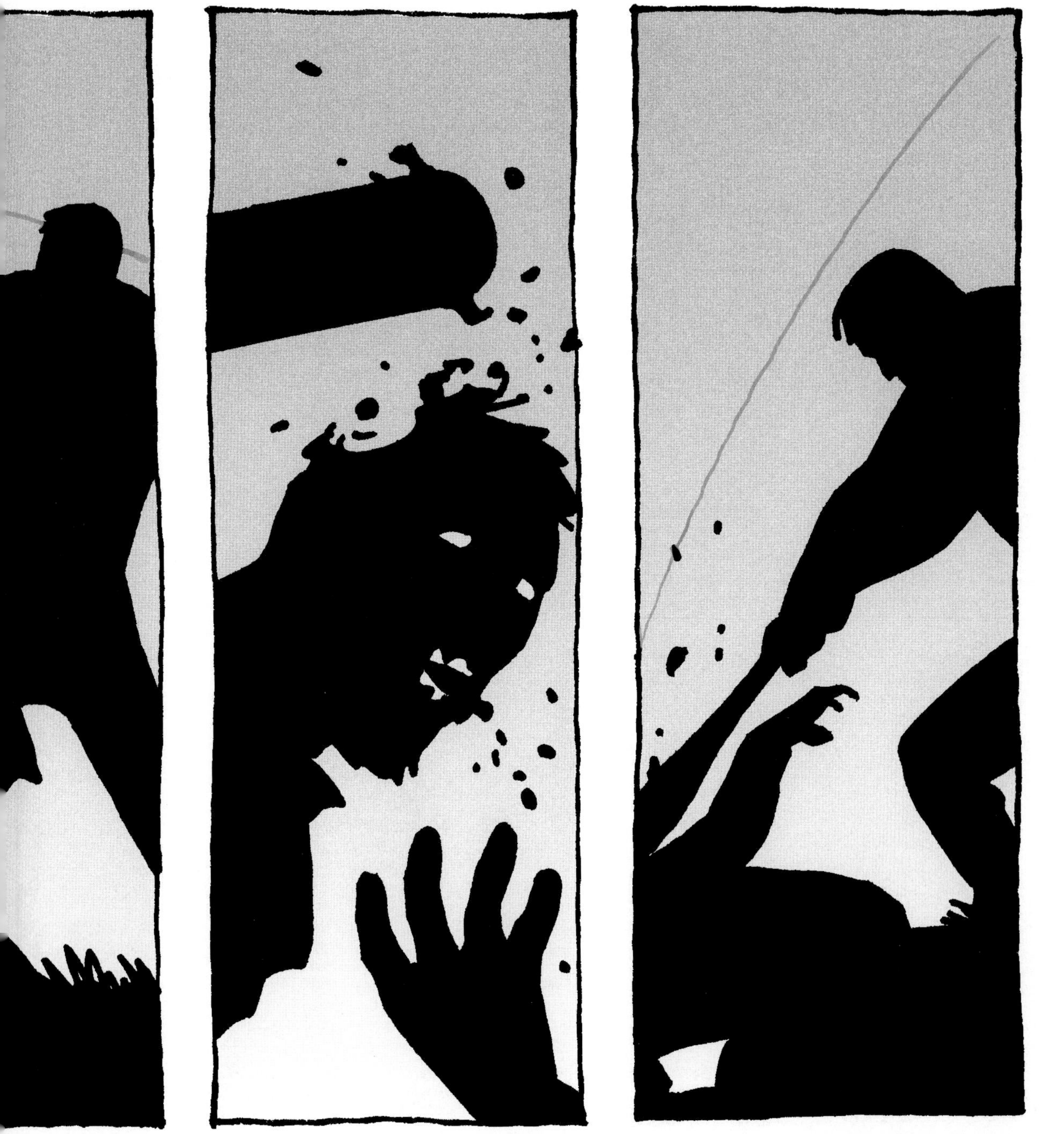
LUCILLE.”

FOR MORE OF THE WALKING DEAD

TRADEPAPERBACKS

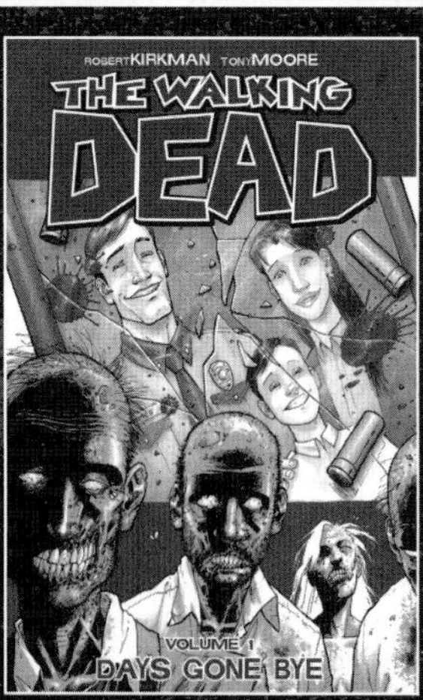

ROBERT KIRKMAN TONY MOORE
THE WALKING DEAD
VOLUME 1
DAYS GONE BYE

VOL. 1: DAYS GONE BYE TP
ISBN: 978-1-58240-672-5
$14.99
VOL. 2: MILES BEHIND US TP
ISBN: 978-1-58240-775-3
$14.99
VOL. 3: SAFETY BEHIND BARS TP
ISBN: 978-1-58240-805-7
$14.99
VOL. 4: THE HEART'S DESIRE TP
ISBN: 978-1-58240-530-8
$14.99
VOL. 5: THE BEST DEFENSE TP
ISBN: 978-1-58240-612-1
$14.99
VOL. 6: THIS SORROWFUL LIFE TP
ISBN: 978-1-58240-684-8
$14.99
VOL. 7: THE CALM BEFORE TP
ISBN: 978-1-58240-828-6
$14.99
VOL. 8: MADE TO SUFFER TP
ISBN: 978-1-58240-883-5
$14.99
VOL. 9: HERE WE REMAIN TP
ISBN: 978-1-60706-022-2
$14.99
VOL. 10: WHAT WE BECOME TP
ISBN: 978-1-60706-075-8
$14.99
VOL. 11: FEAR THE HUNTERS TP
ISBN: 978-1-60706-181-6
$14.99
VOL. 12: LIFE AMONG THEM TP
ISBN: 978-1-60706-254-7
$14.99
VOL. 13: TOO FAR GONE TP
ISBN: 978-1-60706-329-2
$14.99
VOL. 14: NO WAY OUT TP
ISBN: 978-1-60706-392-6
$14.99
VOL. 15: WE FIND OURSELVES TP
ISBN: 978-1-60706-440-4
$14.99
VOL. 16: A LARGER WORLD TP
ISBN: 978-1-60706-559-3
$14.99
VOL. 17: SOMETHING TO FEAR TP
ISBN: 978-1-60706-615-6
$14.99
VOL. 18: WHAT COMES AFTER TP
ISBN: 978-1-60706-687-3
$14.99
VOL. 19: MARCH TO WAR TP
ISBN: 978-1-60706-818-1
$14.99
VOL. 20: ALL OUT WAR PART ONE TP
ISBN: 978-1-60706-882-2
$14.99
VOL. 21: ALL OUT WAR PART TWO TP
ISBN: 978-1-63215-030-1
$14.99
VOL. 22: A NEW BEGINNING TP
ISBN: 978-1-63215-041-7
$14.99
VOL. 23: WHISPERS INTO SCREAMS TP
ISBN: 978-1-63215-258-9
$14.99
VOL. 24: LIFE AND DEATH TP
ISBN: 978-1-63215-402-6
$14.99
VOL. 25: NO TURNING BACK TP
ISBN: 978-1-63215-612-9
$14.99
VOL. 26: CALL TO ARMS TP
ISBN: 978-1-63215-917-5
$14.99
VOL. 27: THE WHISPERER WAR TP
ISBN: 978-1-5343-0052-1
$14.99
VOL. 1: SPANISH EDITION TP
ISBN: 978-1-60706-797-9
$14.99
VOL. 2: SPANISH EDITION TP
ISBN: 978-1-60706-845-7
$14.99
VOL. 3: SPANISH EDITION TP
ISBN: 978-1-60706-883-9
$14.99
VOL. 4: SPANISH EDITION TP
ISBN: 978-1-63215-035-6
$14.99

HARDCOVERS

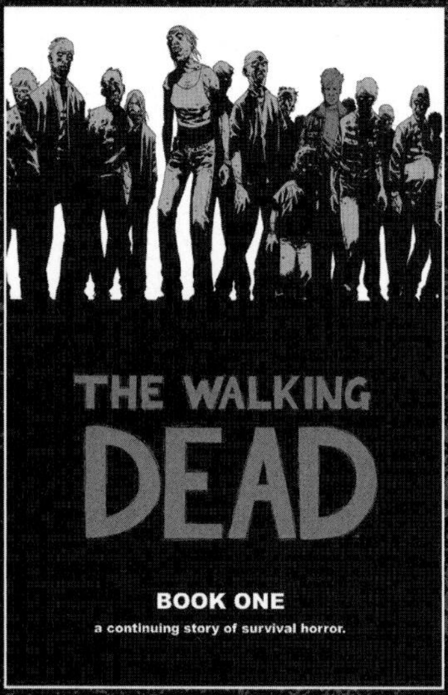

THE WALKING DEAD
BOOK ONE
a continuing story of survival horror.

BOOK ONE HC
ISBN: 978-1-58240-619-0
$34.99
BOOK TWO HC
ISBN: 978-1-58240-698-5
$34.99
BOOK THREE HC
ISBN: 978-1-58240-825-5
$34.99
BOOK FOUR HC
ISBN: 978-1-60706-000-0
$34.99
BOOK FIVE HC
ISBN: 978-1-60706-171-7
$34.99
BOOK SIX HC
ISBN: 978-1-60706-327-8
$34.99
BOOK SEVEN HC
ISBN: 978-1-60706-439-8
$34.99
BOOK EIGHT HC
ISBN: 978-1-60706-593-7
$34.99
BOOK NINE HC
ISBN: 978-1-60706-798-6
$34.99
BOOK TEN HC
ISBN: 978-1-63215-034-9
$34.99
BOOK ELEVEN HC
ISBN: 978-1-63215-271-8
$34.99
BOOK TWELVE HC
ISBN: 978-1-63215-451-4
$34.99
BOOK THIRTEEN HC
ISBN: 978-1-63215-916-8
$34.99

COMPENDIUMS

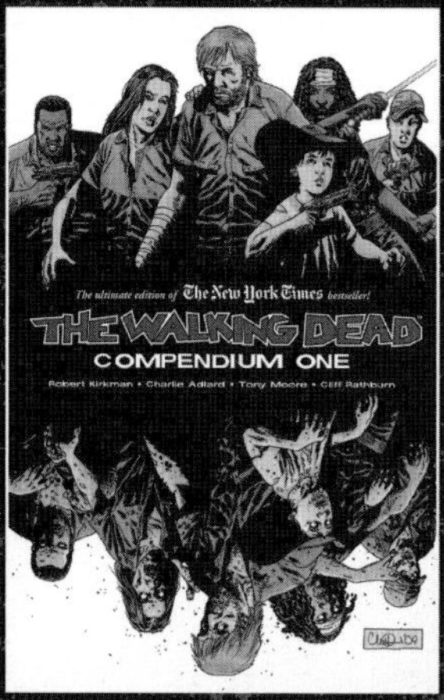

The ultimate edition of The New York Times bestseller!
THE WALKING DEAD
COMPENDIUM ONE
Robert Kirkman • Charlie Adlard • Tony Moore • Cliff Rathburn

COMPENDIUM TP, VOL. 1
ISBN: 978-1-60706-076-5
$59.99
COMPENDIUM TP, VOL. 2
ISBN: 978-1-60706-596-8
$59.99
COMPENDIUM TP, VOL. 3
ISBN: 978-1-63215-456-9
$59.99

SPECIALTY BOOKS

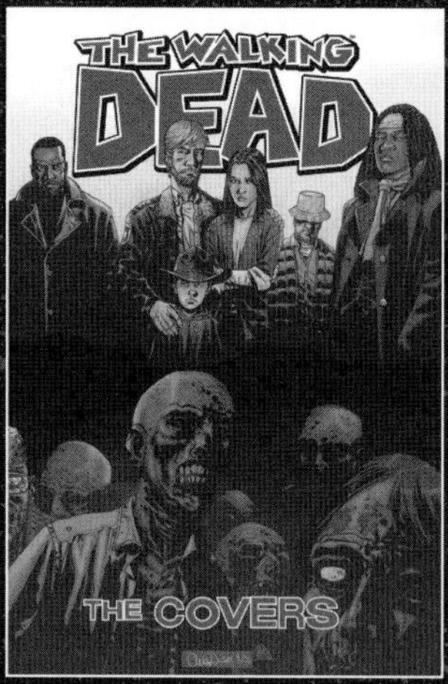

THE WALKING DEAD
THE COVERS

THE WALKING DEAD: THE COVERS, VOL. 1 HC
ISBN: 978-1-60706-002-4
$24.99
THE WALKING DEAD: ALL OUT WAR HC
ISBN: 978-1-63215-038-7
$34.99
THE WALKING DEAD COLORING BOOK
ISBN: 978-1-63215-774-4
$14.99
THE WALKING DEAD RICK GRIMES COLORING BOOK
ISBN: 978-1-5343-0003-3
$14.99

OMNIBUS

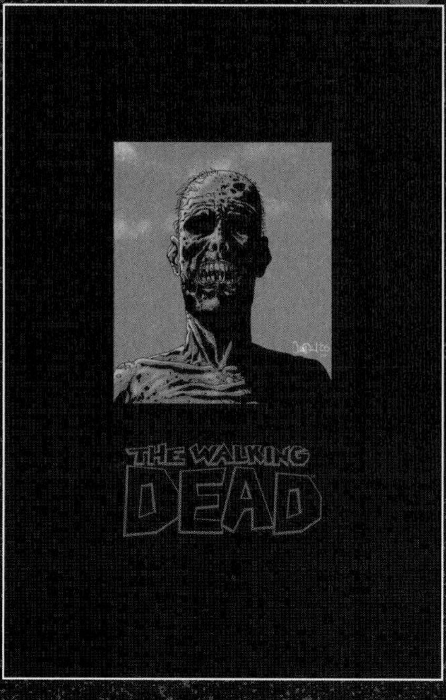

THE WALKING DEAD

OMNIBUS, VOL. 1
ISBN: 978-1-60706-503-6
$100.00
OMNIBUS, VOL. 2
ISBN: 978-1-60706-515-9
$100.00
OMNIBUS, VOL. 3
ISBN: 978-1-60706-330-8
$100.00
OMNIBUS, VOL. 4
ISBN: 978-1-60706-616-3
$100.00
OMNIBUS, VOL. 5
ISBN: 978-1-63215-042-4
$100.00
OMNIBUS, VOL. 6
ISBN: 978-1-63215-521-4
$100.00

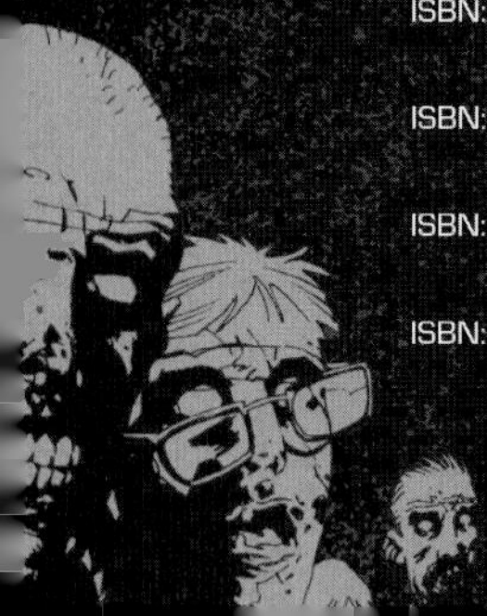

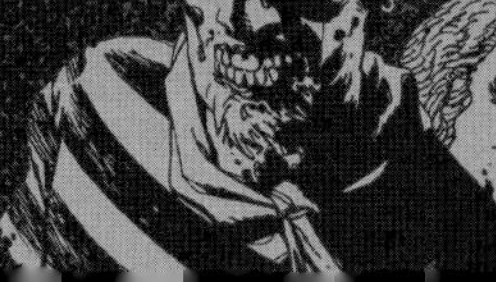